MURDER
IN THE
ROUGH

MURDER IN THE ROUGH

Leslie Allen

COACHWHIP PUBLICATIONS

Greenville, Ohio

To Harry A. Newman, K. C., the best landlord
an author ever had. —L. A.

Murder in the Rough, by Leslie Allen (pseud., Horace Brown)
© 2018 Coachwhip Publications

Published 1946.
No claims made on public domain material.
Cover: Golf ball on grass © Releon8211

CoachwhipBooks.com

ISBN 1-61646-447-X
ISBN-13 978-1-61646-447-9

AN INTRODUCTION

Because I know Napoleon B. Smith so well, I am continually amazed when someone asks me something about the great detective. When a man or an object becomes familiar, it is natural to treat him or it as equally known to all.

In my role as chronicler of the activities of Napoleon B. Smith, I have always attempted a certain objectivity. It is so easy to be carried away with admiration for a man's accomplishments as to become blind to his faults. Thus, if Napoleon B. emerges as a human being in your mind, I am pleased.

Napoleon B. Smith and I first became acquainted when I was a newspaper reporter and he was an acting-detective on the city police force. He gave me a big story on his round-up of a gang of pickpockets. It happened to be a scoop and meant a few dollars more each week in my pay envelope, so we became fast friends.

After the Fairchild murder case, in which Napoleon B. figured so brilliantly and I was once again Johnny on the spot with the news, the detective decided to go into private practice. I wrote a story about how he was interested in solving the famous Amos Smallman disappearance, and, despite the fact that he never did, that yarn got him more publicity than all his successes. While he followed the usual routine of divorce cases and shadowing for small change for a while, he finally got a break by cracking the Amsterdam diamond robbery before the police could get a line on the gang that was behind the job. I wrote the case into a book, *The Amsterdam Diamond Robbery*, and Napoleon B. Smith became famous overnight. He took his fame as a matter of course, as he does everything else.

From then on it was a weird partnership. I tagged Napoleon B. like a setter pup, nosing along with him into all his more spectacular cases, retiring to turn them into book form for what the detective derisively called "my public," while he went on with the routine cases that meant bread-and-butter. Then, perhaps while I would be sleeping the sleep of the author who has finally delivered himself of his brain child, the telephone would ring, and Napoleon B. and I would be off on some further round of adventure.

It's a very nice life, if you can get it . . . and stand it.

Napoleon B. Smith is a lardy man. His bulk is so huge that he often gives the impression of medium height, but he is actually almost six-foot-two. His eyes disappear in his suety face, only to appear suddenly and viciously when he opens them upon a point or object of interest. His voice, as is common with many big and fat men, is high-pitched and almost effeminate. He doesn't like me to say that but it's true, so I risk his displeasure by putting it down once again. Napoleon B. has the flat feet of the man who has pounded a beat for years before getting into civvies, but he can move like lightning for all his bulk and seeming clumsiness. While he does not talk about his youth, and I have never been able to piece it all together, I believe from fragments I have picked up here and there that he was once a very fast and shifty linesman and clever at first base.

Everything about Napoleon B. Smith shrieks policeman, and of this he is proud. He claims that his early training and discipline, the thorough grounding he received in all phases of police work, his special course with the F.B.I. at Washington, and his contacts with police officials all over North America—all have been invaluable to him. But he is sufficient of an egotist to recognize that these trainings have but been added to a very shrewd mind and a bulldog attention to detail that make him one of the greatest criminologists of his generation. When he walks along the street, you think of him as a policeman off duty. Those who have had the misfortune to have had him on their misguided trails have thought of him as Doom.

Napoleon B. lives in sublime and sweaty bachelorhood, scornful of the fact that I am a prey for every pretty face. Our rooms are the most untidy I have ever seen, but, apart from the constant cascade of perspiration pouring down his face, he is always faultlessly turned out, a habit no doubt of his uniformed days. He has one passion in life, and one only; he will walk a mile on aching feet for ice cream, never less than three dishes, often a half-dozen, with the odd banana split sandwiched in for relief from the white expanses of frozen delight. No matter how his doctor rails against this practice, Napoleon B. continues to eat ice cream. He always says it's insurance; the Devil will never be able to thaw him out. I firmly believe that the nearest he came to letting a criminal slip through his fingers was when that clever Doctor Arnheim tried to bribe him with strawberry flavor.

The question I am most asked is: "Does the B. in Napoleon B. stand for Bonaparte?"

That's one mystery Napoleon B. has never solved for me. The only time I ever asked him, he scowled at me, said very shortly, "Buttercup!" and went back to spooning his ice cream.

The detective has always, I feel, had a soft spot in his heart for the mystery I call *Murder in the Rough*. This is because not only was he, and he alone, responsible for solution of the crime . . . he was also responsible for its discovery.

I like the case myself because of its sidelights on human frailty, and for its unusual background. To a confirmed golfer like myself, there's something almost sporting about *Murder in the Rough*.

Leslie Allen.

CHAPTER ONE

The sun bounced hotly from the first tee of the exclusive new Briar Hill course, glazing the green fairway over with a faint haze, a fairway that seemed to stretch into the infinite but was really only three hundred and forty yards of grassy straits, bounded by the Scylla and Charybdis of tree-infested, rock-strewn rough. A few flies buzzed with lackless determination about a chocolate wrapper some careless member had thrown away instead of depositing in the receptacle placed pointedly beside each tee. In the verdant distance the red flag on the green barely found enough energy to wave at us. With the hands of my watch showing nine o'clock of a perfect golfing morning, Napoleon B. Smith and I sat on the bench and waited for the boy to set up my ball. The detective's caddy industriously scrubbed Napoleon B.'s grassy and scratched ball between ingeniously-placed brushes while he waited his turn to tee up.

Everything pointed to a wonderful eighteen holes before noon on a brand-new course where we had been admitted only because one of Napoleon B's clients had been so grateful as to forget that the rich cannot afford to be generous. The new Briar Hill course was championship plus and so

snooty its waiters had to use periscopes to see where they
were going. For one like myself who shot in the low eighties,
it should have been paradise. It should have been—but it
wasn't. The sour note in the symphonie de golf was Napoleon B. Smith.

There are poor golfers and there are bad golfers, and then
there are men who call themselves golfers but who should
be sued for libel by the custodians of the royal and ancient
game. In the last class is Napoleon B. Smith. Yet, like so
many of the breed, he fancied himself as a peerless player, a
golfer whose name should rank with Bobby Jones. Rank is
right, for Napoleon B. went around in the low nineties, that
is, for nine holes; after that he stopped counting.

To make matters worse, from my long-suffering view-
point, the detective could have been a great golfer. His
drives were tremendous. I've seldom seen him tee off less
than two hundred and fifty yards and I am telling the truth
when I say that he was more often close to three-fifty. But
all these terrific drives were wasted, for they were accompa-
nied by (a) an unbelievable slice, or (b) a miraculous hook.
The roughs, where Napoleon B. spends at least sixty per
cent of his golfing time, are always blue. In the same way his
iron shots seldom go less than two hundred yards, always
managing to overshoot the green. When he four-putts, it's
a miracle. There's always a sand-storm when he's in a trap.

I have never known the detective to take the blame for
anything in a game of golf. It's always the so-and-so caddy,
or the blankety-blank ball, or the blasted weather, or anything else that happens to be handy . . . *never* Napoleon B.
Smith.

Golf, as played by Napoleon B. Smith, is a vice. It in-
duces in him varied forms of lying and cheating, such as
a complete inability to add up his score properly or to

remember that he took fourteen strokes on the third hole. His card invariably bristles with fours and fives, with here and there a judiciously placed three. On a short hole, where he's taken eight, I've known him to sneak in a two.

Which is not to say Napoleon B. Smith is not otherwise a solid citizen. He is just the perfect dub.

You will understand, therefore, why I could not enjoy the beauties of the morning. I was even more disturbed by the fact that Napoleon B. Smith was "singing." The quotes will be obvious to anyone who has ever heard him. It was the *Rangers' Song* from *Rio Rita*, and I gripped hard at the bench in order to avoid bashing him with my driver.

"Do you *have* to sing, Napoleon B.?" I demanded, speaking low so my caddy wouldn't hear me.

"Why not?" The big goof beamed about him fatuously. "It's a day to make a donkey sing!"

I agreed with feeling, but he was blissfully unaware.

"I feel so good!" he caroled. "The usual dollar-a-hole, I suppose?"

I nodded resignedly and said, "The usual dollar-a-hole. And look, Napoleon B., please, when a ball's lost and you've looked for it five minutes, give it up, won't you, please, for my sake?"

My tones should have melted the Sphinx, but Napoleon B. Smith glared at me. "What!" he thundered, "and lose a stroke? Nothing doing! You're always trying to get the best of me, Les, but class tells, doesn't it?"

Not being able to answer that one, I picked up my driver, looked at his hulk reflectively, thought better of it, and ambled over to the tee. It was going to be one hell of a day, I could see that.

As I looked down the fairway, however, my troubles seemed very small ones. It was a beautiful day, one of the finest of a lovely spring. We had the course practically to ourselves, which was an advantage because Napoleon B. is a slow golfer. I tried the feel of the club, and it was true. The caddy stepped back respectfully, while I admonished him to keep his eye on the ball, and addressed myself to a practice swing. It was ruined by Napoleon B. bursting into his own peculiar rendition of *Rolling Down to Rio*. He broke off as I completed my wobbly swing.

"Missed it entirely," he said unctuously.

I turned on him blisteringly, but he was gazing innocently off into space.

"You know damn well that was only a practice stroke," I said, "and anyway, how could anybody drive with you making that confounded noise?"

He looked injured, and asked with dignity if I was referring to his singing. I said that I was, if that was what he wanted to call it, and the exchange ended up, as did most of our verbal bouts, with him chuckling and me grinning lopsidedly because I couldn't help it. The detective waved his big hand genially at the tee and I turned back with a shrug of my shoulders. For a miracle he was quiet, and I got away a beauty, a clean, hard-smacking drive that went two-fifty like an arrow down the fairway.

"You had a string on that one, Les," said Napoleon B. magnanimously. "Now watch me."

"And you watch the ball," I admonished. "Keep your eye on it as though it were a pickpocket. Don't let it out of your sight."

Napoleon B. was waddling towards his teed-up ball as I spoke. The little white pill looked so small and dainty beside him, I smiled to myself at the contrast.

"There're more silly darn rules to this game," he threw at me over his shoulder. "Me, I play it my own way and I get there just the same. Here, I'll show you what I mean."

He didn't even look where the ball was, I swear it. He gave one of those convulsive heaves of his, the driver punched hard enough at his ball to flatten it, and I watched dismally as the screaming ball "tailed" away in a wonderful hook, heading for the rough with all the precision of a bird dog. Napoleon B's eyes followed it with the usual child-like unbelief. It was at least three-twenty-five and into a clump of trees.

An expletive of heroic dimensions in Napoleon B's high-pitched voice startled the caddy, who dropped the detective's bag with a clatter. Napoleon B. gave him a look that said it was all the caddy's fault, and strode off down the fairway without looking back at me. I followed sadly.

Well, that's the way our golf went. You couldn't rightly call it a game. A game is something at which you have fun. But I was wishing miserably I was anywhere else but Briar Hill, preferably the middle of the Pacific Ocean, and Napoleon B. became grimmer and grimmer as the match progressed. That's the way it always went. Along about the third hole the detective would lose his heartiness and *sang-froid*. He would become an implacable man-mountain, fighting relentlessly against the forces of nature and the devil he conceived as bearing down upon him.

Not that I did not have reason to be happy. I had negotiated the first six holes in two over par, and was angry enough to possibly set an all-time record for myself by closing the gap and finishing in the middle seventies. If I could negotiate the seventh hole in par, I told myself, I could make up those two strokes and be the first man over the Briar Hill course in par. It was enough to make me forget Napoleon B. Smith.

Except for the seventh hole.

The seventh hole at Briar Hill was designed by some man who was peeved at his mother-in-law and wanted to take it out on the rest of the world. It is a steep, five hundred and twenty yard "dog-leg"—that is, a long hole bent in the middle like a dog's leg, and going off at right angles to its original course. There's an extremely narrow fairway and wicked roughs on either side. The only way to play it is cautiously. Iron your first shot straight off the tee for about one-seventy-five and you won't have any particular trouble with the par five.

It being my perpetual "honor," that's exactly what I did. Then Napoleon B. teed up. I shut my eyes, knowing instinctively what he would do.

He did!

Another three feet, perhaps, and his ball would have cleared the wilderness of trees and brush and sailed gaily onto the dog-leg of the fairway, confounding all my expectations. That three feet meant all the difference between Napoleon B's happiness and constant self-reproach. We couldn't know that at the time.

But the needed three feet was missing, and the ball disappeared swiftly into the tangle below. Napoleon B. looked at me, his red face scarlet.

"If you say one word of 'I told you so,'" he said ominously, "I'll take this expensive club and wrap it 'round your neck."

"You can't stop me from thinking," I retorted, and added desperately, "Look, Chief, there's a slow foursome behind us. If we have to let them play through we won't be home to go to bed. Play another one off, and forget about that shot. You'll never find the ball in that jungle."

"And be playing three? Nothing doing!"

"All right," I said, "we'll forget you've already played a shot, and you can start over."

"And cheat!" Napoleon B's indignation was superb enough to be real. "Leslie, I'm surprised at you. You know I always count all my strokes."

What can a person do against a setup like that? I did the only thing I could: followed Napoleon B. and his caddy, while motioning my boy to stand by my ball in case somebody wanted to pick it up. From past experience I knew Napoleon B. would bloodhound that ball until he found it.

"You find that ball, caddy," said the fat man expansively, "and I'll give you a dollar."

"Yes, sir!" The caddy was eager. "I'll find it."

"Hmmm . . . well, I may have spoken a bit hastily. Let's make that two bits, shall we, huh?"

Which should give you another slant on the many-slanted Napoleon B. Smith, and make you wonder why I love the cuss better than a brother. I'm coming to that.

The spot into which Napoleon B's fast-traveling ball bad dropped had been known in the neighborhood for a good many years before a golf course was even thought about as *Hell's Half-Acre*. Of all the forsaken places one can imagine, this stretch of green wilderness, choked with the natural debris of Time, perhaps comes closest to a golfer's idea of Dante's nethermost nether region. Only a parsimonious and obstinate man like Napoleon B. Smith would even think of looking for a ball in there.

As we descended into the depths, where even the bright sunlight of that singularly lovely day had difficulty in penetrating, my spirits oozed farther and farther down into my boots. I had that psychic feeling of impending danger or trouble at which Napoleon B. laughs so heartily and upon which he relies so much.

There was a path of sorts, which we followed. It must have been some sort of misguided lovers' lane, for only lovers and golfers would have been fools enough to prowl these leafed-in tunnels.

And yet there was an air of wild beauty to the place. We had not gone many steps into it before we seemed in another world. Everyday sounds were muted; birds seemed far away and lonely; even the dead branches that snapped under our feet did so with a sort of a deprecatory little cough. It was like the places we read about in *Grimm's Fairy Tales*, where the forest closes in behind the children as they walk, but withal quietly and not arousing terror until too late. Even Napoleon B. Smith seemed to sense that here was an ageless calm, and when he crashed his elephantine way ahead he did so apologetically.

We spread out fan-wise. Involuntarily, I wished I had a machete. That's what I had been reminded of: the Faversham case, and the Brazilian jungle. There was something . . . but this was the United States, and . . .

"Let's give up," I called out, and the dense foliage muffled my words.

"Give up!" I could imagine the outraged look Napoleon B. was pouring my way. "That's a good ball. Besides, what kind of a detective am I if I can't find a golf ball? Caddy, which way did you line that ball up?"

I heard the caddy say something about "lined it up with that tree over there," and marveled at the skill of caddies and their ways of finding a little ball in a huge expanse.

We hunted for what seemed an hour but must have been only another ten minutes. By that time, even the slow foursome would have been able to play through us. It was cool in there after the hot sun, and I shivered. There was something in the air that added to the unreasoning spasm.

A few yards away, I heard Napoleon B. give a yell of triumph.

"Here's my ball!" he shouted. "Here it is! And a perfect lie."

Obviously the caddy had come over and looked, for the boy said, "That's not your ball, Mr. Smith. That's a *Nonsuch 4*. You were playing a *Superlastic*."

"I was, eh?" I heard Napoleon B. growl, and then add with great cheerfulness, "Oh well, it's a good ball. Hardly nicked at all. Put it in my bag, Fred."

It was while I turned away from the sounds with a chuckle that had its admixture of annoyance that I saw it. It was a *Superlastic*, all right.

For some moments I debated what to do. More than anyone else, I knew Napoleon B's peculiar sensitivity. You'd think him a man with a hide like an ox, but I've seen his eyes fill with tears at the sight of a man hobbling along on crutches. He had a positive hatred for hurting anything unless in the line of duty.

I knew what I had to do. It was unavoidable, but it was necessary. I couldn't leave it there.

"I've found it, Napoleon B.," I called, but my voice was cracked and hollow. "It's right over this way."

He crashed through to my side, as happy as any child who has rediscovered a favorite toy.

"Good old Les!" he yelled. "Where is it? Is it a good lie?"

His eyes followed my pointing finger, and his high voice exclaimed.

It was an extremely bad lie . . . unless winter rules apply to dead bodies!

CHAPTER TWO

In police work of a certain type, death is commonplace. It becomes routine, much like taking a street car in the morning or going to the movies once a week. But nobody ever really becomes hardened to death in civilian life, where it is unexpected and unwanted.

When you looked at her, your mind said "Grandmother." She was sweet and gentle in appearance, a sweetness and a gentleness that death could not hide or had been too recent to erase these marks of life. Her body was tiny and frail, and there was an air of repose about the aging features as though what had come had come with swift stealing and had caused no alarm. She lay half-hidden in the underbrush, and by her side, in short line with her head and as white as her hair, was Napoleon B's unmistakable *Superlastic* golf ball.

There could have been a count of five before either one of us moved. Then I turned away, unable to bear the tragic look on Napoleon B's homely face.

"I didn't mean to do it," he said finally, and very slowly. "It was an accident."

"Of course it was," I soothed. "It could have happened to anybody."

Napoleon B. is too honest with himself in a crisis.

"No, it couldn't have!" he said fiercely. "It could only happen to a pig-headed fool like me. You told me not to drive through here, but I was bound and determined . . . and now look what I've done."

Fred, the caddy, had come up by this time and was standing beside us, not saying anything, just looking, his young eyes big and round with their first glimpse of sudden death and a pallor on his baby face that spelt fainting if I didn't find something for him to do. I thought of something.

"Fred," I told him, "Dr. Bryce is in that foursome that was behind us. Get him."

The lad was intelligent and glad to get away from that place. He ran for the open, tripped over a half-hidden log, picked himself up and stumbled out of our sight.

"Bryce?" Napoleon B. raised his great head and looked at me dismally. "You mean the coroner?"

I nodded. Napoleon B. sagged visibly. I put my hand upon the beef of his arm consolingly, but he shook it away.

Dr. Thomas Bryce was annoyed. He was a fussy little man of the type I dislike, but competent in his office and respected in his profession. A man who wears a pince-nez is always suspect with me, especially if he carries the affectation to the absurd length of sporting it in a golf game. But I must admit he took charge of the situation admirably.

As soon as he saw the old lady he grunted in recognition. Doctors like Bryce never seem to be shocked by death. It isn't callousness or indifference; it's a needed cloak for true feelings. A doctor would be in a perpetual state of sorrow if he allowed his outer life to obtrude to his inner.

Bending down, Bryce made a hasty examination. Even I could tell it was a matter of form.

"She's still warm," he said, more to himself than to us. "What happened?"

"You're the doctor," I flipped, and he shot me a glance that scorched.

"I was under that impression, Mr. Allen." He swept a look around all of us and seized upon Napoleon B's silent misery. "What seems to be the trouble, Mr. Smith?"

Napoleon B. pointed reluctantly to the golf ball.

"I realize you found her beside the golf ball." Dr. Bryce was impatient. After all, his game had been disturbed, and he was a man who took his golf seriously. "However, I don't know what you're driving at. This is obviously a case of heart failure."

The detective roused himself long enough to ask, "Why obviously?"

"What else could it be?"

"I could have killed her," Napoleon B. said glumly.

The doctor's jaw fell open a full inch. He stared with disbelief at the detective. Then a dull flush slipped over his pale face. "This scarcely seems a time for joking," he said irritably.

"I wish I *were* joking." The fat man turned so that he could not see the body even out of the corner of his eye. "She was walking along here. My ball came down hard. Bingo! I guess it's open-and-shut."

After a good two or three seconds, Dr. Bryce said reluctantly, "Well, you're a detective, Napoleon B. But I'm damned sorry about this."

"You needn't think I'm not."

"Oh, don't worry about a thing. It's a pure case of accidental death."

I couldn't help putting in maliciously, "I thought you said it was heart failure."

Napoleon B. waved me off. He knew I was saying things I shouldn't have, for his sake. We understood each other that way.

His high-pitched voice had a decided break in it. "I wouldn't listen to Les. I *had* to do it *my* way. I *had* to shoot over those trees . . . only the ball didn't go over."

Bryce called the shaking caddy over to him. "Run up to the clubhouse, Fred," he said, "and tell Mr. Williams what's happened. Tell him to keep it quiet, but he can bring Joe and a stretcher and we'll get the old lady out of here. Then run back to my foursome and tell Mr. Johnson what's holding me up. Tell him to go ahead without me. Here's a dollar."

"No, no." Napoleon B. waved the doctor's hand away from his pocket. "I'll pay it."

And he did. It shows how miserable he was feeling.

"Now," Bryce went on briskly, "about this nonsense of your having killed the old lady, Napoleon B., forget it. It was a pure accident."

A leaf fell on the old lady's still face and Napoleon B. winced as though someone had hit him. He bent and brushed it off with an unaccustomed tenderness.

"If I hadn't driven my ball in here, she'd be alive this minute."

The coroner was impatient. "This woman was a patient of mine." He snapped the words at the fat man. "She suffered from coronary thrombosis. She'd have gone off at any time."

Napoleon B. shook his head, unconvinced. I lost patience with him myself.

"Oh, for Pete's sake," I told him bluntly, "quit having fun by making a martyr of yourself."

He gave me a look filled with such genuine reproach that I realized with misgiving how real was his grief. The fat man actually believed he had killed the old girl, killed her as though he had taken a stick and knocked her down with a fatal blow.

"Come on back to the clubhouse," I said. "You'll only worry yourself into a decline standing around here."

"I want to help carry her back, Leslie." Napoleon B. called me "Leslie" only in times of great emotional stress. "It's the least I can do."

It's no use arguing with a talent for misery like that. I sought to divert the detective's attention by asking Bryce who she had been.

"That's Mrs. Joshua Cartwright," said the M. D., nodding a little callously at the body. "Maybe you've heard of her."

"The name's certainly familiar." I concentrated for a moment. "Picture in the newspaper. Story in the morgue at the *Herald*. Money. Wait a minute! I've got it! Isn't this her golf course?"

Bryce nodded. "You've a remarkable memory, Mr. Allen," he conceded rather acidly. I don't think Bryce ever liked me any more than I liked him. "And you're quite right. Mrs. Cartwright did own this golf course, much to her regret."

Napoleon B. was interested in spite of himself, as I knew he would be. You always let a hungry lion smell raw meat.

"What do you mean, Doc, 'much to her regret'?" he asked.

The coroner didn't like being called "Doc." Most doctors don't, as a matter of fact.

"She was eccentric," he snapped. "Very eccentric."

"You mean," I said, "if she'd been poor instead of rich she'd have been confined in an institution?"

"Something like that." The coroner, with more thoughtfulness than I would have given him credit, took off his gaudy sweater and laid it over the dead woman's face. It really didn't seem decent to discuss her, as we were doing, while her wide-open eyes stared at us with rigid uncomprehension. "Her husband left her millions, but I'm afraid she never enjoyed them. Her tastes were simple. Some would have called them simple-mindedness."

Somewhere, in another world, a robin called shrilly to its mate. The sound, in this leafed-over grave, was unnatural.

"For instance?" I prompted, noting warily that some of the strain in Napoleon B's face had been replaced by the interest he always showed in the quirks of humanity. The detective, given other opportunities, would have been a worldfamous psychiatrist, perhaps blazing new paths in that still little-explored territory. As it is, he is one of the finest amateur psychologists I have ever known.

"Well," continued the doctor, and I think he was on to my game, "for instance, there's this place."

"I wondered about that," put in Napoleon B., coming alive. "She hardly seems the type to have been looking for lost golf balls."

His own crack rebounded unfortunately on suddenly-sobered features.

"No." There was something of a twinkle in Bryce's sharp eyes, and I almost liked him for once. "This land used to belong to her."

"Used to?"

"It was part of her dowry. An old-fashioned arrangement. Joshua Cartwright was what is known as a 'hard man.' I believe he married Mary for the little money and estate she could bring him. This land was part of a parcel her father left her. While she still loved him, Cartwright had her deed the land to him. Some years ago he sold it for a golf course, but the place wasn't opened in his lifetime."

"Why not?" pursued Napoleon B., and Bryce flushed again. I remembered he was usually the one to ask the questions, in his capacity as coroner.

"Some little hidden shame in Joshua's mind. He stipulated when he sold the land that it was not to be used for its present purpose for five years. He knew his wife loved the place; not the whole thing, but this part called *Hell's Half-Acre*. It was part of her eccentricity, and yet I wonder."

I wondered what he wondered, and asked him.

"Whether she was not the one who was right, and we are the poorer for believing her wrong. Some years ago she read Hudson's *Green Mansions*. It made a tremendous impression upon her."

"Me, too," said Napoleon B. surprisingly. "I thought it one of the best books of the Twentieth Century. Once you've read about the birdlike Rima other romances seem stale."

"Such as the Lady of the Camellias?" I couldn't resist the snide remark, a bit baffled by this unsuspected literacy in the fat man's make-up, as I am continually baffled by the maze that is his mind.

"Tepid and wishy-washy in comparison," snorted Napoleon B., unaware of the rib. "Never could stand Armand."

That was too much. I shut up, while the doctor went on, after lifting his eyebrow in Smith's direction and smiling his odd little secretive smile.

"As I said, she read the great naturalist's book, and I think in her own mind she romantically identified herself with Rima, and longed to go roaming down the green world of Brazil finding the happiness life had denied her. At any rate, she conceived an overwhelming passion for Nature. Of course, she was too old to go tramping up to the headwaters of the Amazon, so she turned this place here into a sort of wild-plant sanctuary. She actually paid a lot of money to try to grow jungle flowers, like orchids, but without success. Then her husband sold the place over her head, mostly, I think, because it was the one thing left that gave her happiness." He sighed heavily, twisting his pince-nez absent-mindedly. "Joshua Cartwright was a hard man, a practical man, and he was impatient, very impatient, of anything he did not understand."

Something clicked with me. "It's coming back," I said rapidly, so that I wouldn't lose the thought. "Didn't this louse of a Cartwright try to have her committed to an asylum?"

Dr. Bryce looked at me in surprise. "Why no," he answered. "At least, not that I'm aware."

"Oh." I was disappointed in my memory. It very seldom lets me down. "There's something about her. Wait! I've got it! Cartwright died suddenly about . . . yes, about a year ago."

"That's right. He was drowned from his yacht. An experienced sailor, too. I always told him he overate, but he never would listen to advice from anyone. What he paid me for, I can't understand. He was as healthy as any man I've ever known."

Napoleon B. spoke slowly, "I suppose she was glad he died."

"Yes, I suppose she was," said the coroner with some surprise. "Poor Mary! You know, I wouldn't be surprised if the will directed us to bury her here in her *Green Mansions*."

I looked at my watch. It was three minutes to eleven. I was just about to say, "Time they were getting here," when I heard them coming down the path, and checked myself. It's no fun saying the obvious.

The club manager, a flat-faced, expressionless man named Williams, and Joe, a husky locker room attendant, expressed something that might have passed for sympathy in monosyllables. Then they hefted the slight body to the stretcher none too gently. Napoleon B. took an angry step forward, stopped himself, saw that he would not be needed to help carry that light weight, turned away and went up the dim path alone.

We followed him, a little procession of Death, taking Mary Cartwright for the last time from the peace she loved to the world outside she had been made to hate.

Bringing up the rear, I looked back once. It was very still and cool in *Hell's Half-Acre*.

CHAPTER THREE

In the weather-beaten old courthouse there was a larger assembly than usual for a coroner's jury that promises a routine verdict of accidental death. But the prominence of the protagonists, both dead and alive, plus the elegant spectacle of high-spun relatives in specious mourning served to play the morbid drama to an overflow audience.

Dr. Bryce, in his pin-stripe blue serge business suit, a blue that was almost black, with his hair carefully combed and his pince-nez in position for assault upon the witnesses, was a different person from the grumbling golfer of two days before. He sat, removed from the rest, upon the high bench and I could not help reflect, as I gazed at him and at the plain and ordinary jurors, fidgeting solemnly in their hard chairs, how correct are our courts and how far removed from reality. Yet, as a newspaper reporter, I had seen this clumsy machinery creak along its various highways to an invariable Justice too often to despise it for its weakness and its *chi chi*.

A coroner's court, to the legal mind, is the essence of familiarity and simplicity. The pickup jury is there simply to return a verdict as to the cause and nature of the death, acting upon the instructions of the qualified medical practitioner, for the moment wearing legal status. The antiquated system saves a lot of time and expense to the state.

As the first witness, I told of the finding of the body. The coroner questioned me as to Napoleon B. Smith's golf ball, and then I stepped down, bored with the whole proceedings except insofar as they affected Napoleon B's state of mind. This latter, even after the interval of two days, bordered on a state of mental collapse. I could understand it, I could sympathize with it, but this unsuspected sensitivity on the part of the large man, a sensitivity which my wisest cracks couldn't penetrate, had left me impatient and depressed. After all, accidents will happen.

With one half my mind, I listened to the evidence. The coroner, as the family physician, certified that death was due to heart failure induced by shock, that an autopsy was unnecessary, that a large bruise he had found on the old lady's forehead, near the temple, *could* have been the cause of this shock, and that the bruise—this with obvious reluctance—*could* have been caused by the golf ball which was found lying by the body. Mumble-mumble. Drone-drone. I yawned. I always yawn in courts. It's the closeness of the atmosphere, I guess.

The other half of my mind followed my eyes in wandering over the courtroom. I looked at a fly climbing the nearby dirty window. Then I lowered my sights to a more agreeable object, a very pretty and upset young lady. Having, from force of habit, descended yesterday upon the morgue of the *Herald*, and having digested the complete and voluminous Cartwright file, I knew her for Gale Cartwright, the stepdaughter of the dead woman. Joshua had been married twice and, from what I could read between the lines, should have been married more often than that.

The girl was following every word that was spoken with a fist-clenched intentness. In the half-light from the window I could see that her Indian-dark cheeks were swollen, as though from a great deal of crying. She was dressed neatly in a suit that shrieked money, and she fitted the clothes in a way that my exacting bachelor eye approved. I couldn't see her legs, but I knew they would be good.

She must have felt my intent gaze, because she half-turned suddenly and caught me in the act. My neck got hot in a hurry. I tried a smile but there was no answering smile, even in her eyes. She swiveled back, giving me as cold a brush-off as I have ever had, and I have had more than my share.

I wouldn't, I thought, like to make a mistake with *that* lady.

Sitting next to her was a man who looked much older, but I now knew to be younger. He was Jack Cartwright, Mrs. Cartwright's stepson. He was a no-good, if the morgue clippings were right, and proud of it. There had been a couple of cases with young girls and some vague references to a withdrawn check. Obviously a nasty chip off the old block.

Young Cartwright was slouched back on the scarred wooden bench, his pouchy eyes closed, his hands resting nervously on his knees. He appeared not to be listening, but I had enough courtroom savvy to know that he was taking in every word.

Two benches away I located Cyrus Handley, an extremely good-looking young man, who was frowning amiably into space. He was highly regarded by the morgue—his file was quite heavy and all in his favor. He was North American skeets champion, a successful manufacturer of small arms, including some adaptations of high-powered German compressed-air rifles, and an active leader in boys' work.

Unmarried, the number of clippings from the society page showed him to be one of the best catches in town. Handley was the only other Cartwright relative—a nephew of Mrs. Cartwright, which accounted for the fact that he had none of the hardness of old Joshua about him. Neither, apparently, did the girl, Gale, except for that look she had given me, and she could hardly be blamed for that.

Before I found a blonde to admire I took in the fact that Adam Johnson was also present. He was the Cartwright lawyer, a tall, preposterously thin man, who looked as though he suffered from duodenal ulcers. His bald head and loose-skin features, his long hands peeping from frayed coat cuffs, and the painfully double-jointed way in which he sat made him seem something of a Bolger-like scarecrow, but he had restless gray eyes and I knew his mind was like a steel trap. Napoleon B. and I had run into him on several cases and he had proven a first-rate defense lawyer, once going so far as to convince a jury that a client of his was innocent, after Napoleon B. thought he had him sewn up tight in a black cap ready for the hangman. It was one of the detective's few failures, but he had held a grudging admiration for Johnson ever since.

There was little reason to make such a fuss over the old girl, I told myself, as I winked at the blonde and received a frozen stare that cracked in the middle into an unexpected smile. Poor old Mrs. Cartwright had been worth millions, but she should have been in an institution. No person in her right mind would have spent most of her time down in *Hell's Half-Acre*. Or would she? Was Mrs. Cartwright right, and the rest of us wrong? Did her simple plan of life—a life where love of growing and living was important—did this plan have more sense in it than a world where war and disease and selfishness and cruelty were felt so often that they shocked no longer? Had the old lady not escaped into something finer than . . .

I swear I didn't snore. Napoleon B. says I did, but he likes to rib me. At any rate, in that half-world I had entered I heard a voice I knew to be Bryce's say harshly, "Constable, wake that man up over there. This courtroom is not for sleeping."

Almost before the constable dug me in the ribs with a heavy forefinger, I knew it was me. I knew, too, that my ears were red.

Before I could stop myself, I said, with a rising inflection that broke ludicrously, "Who? Me?"

"Yes, you!" Bryce cracked it out. "If you did not have the good sense to sleep in your own bed last night, at least please have the decency to stay awake here. Continue with the witness, please."

A quickly stifled titter edged around the courtroom. In that moment I swore to get even with Dr. Bryce sometime, somewhere, somehow, if it was the last thing I ever did.

Gale Cartwright was testifying in a tear-dried voice that her stepmother made a visit to *Hell's Half-Acre*, usually at the same time each day. Mrs. Cartwright had always been methodical. On the stand Gale Cartwright was more interestingly pale than ever, and I had been right—her legs were good. A man of my experience can usually tell what a girl's legs will look like from the type of face she is wearing.

I didn't dare look at the blonde again for fear Bryce would pounce on me for that. The constable had his eye on me, too, a quite judicial and impartial eye that said he'd been looking for a chance for years to help a reporter break a leg.

And the evidence was definitely not worth my experienced ear. I had a notion for a moment that it would be fun to suddenly start yapping like a dog. That would really stir old Brice up. But I had no desire to spend the night in the clink, and, as is usual with such uninhibited impulses, the idea died in conception.

The evidence, such as it was, was all in, and Bryce summed up in his dry way. I had to grudgingly admit that the man had a very orderly and logical mind. The way he put it to that jury, if I hadn't been on the spot I still could have seen the old lady lying there, the golf ball nearby, and so on, and so on.

Napoleon B. was sitting up, straight and big in his chair, his whole huge frame rigid. Mounting from his neck, as the dry voice of the coroner went on, was a beautiful shade of purplish red. He was clasping and unclasping his hands on his knees. You never can tell about the hardest of men; they'll kill or torture or maim with a smile on their lips, and cry over their pet canary coming down with pneumonia.

The jury retired, although it really wasn't necessary; the dopes could have come to a verdict right there in their seats. Everyone except Napoleon B. relaxed when the jury went out. Some went outside for a smoke. I caught the blonde looking at me from the corner of her eye, but then the big guy beside her turned and spoke to her and I decided he looked too big and mean to take a chance. I went back to a furtive examination of the Cartwright clan.

After about five minutes the jury filed back in, look-ing sheepish, as though aware its big-shottishness had been noted by everyone. Dr. Bryce was notified and came with quick steps to the bench, his nervous eyes darting around the courtroom, his sarcastic mouth set and hard.

"Have you reached a verdict, gentlemen?" he snapped, practically sneering it.

"We have, Mr. Coroner," replied the foreman, a pomp-ous little man with moustache to match.

"State it."

The foreman cleared his throat, unaccustomed as he was to public speaking, and said, "We, the jury, find that the deceased, Mrs. Joshua Cartwright, came to her death when accidentally struck by a golf ball driven by Mr. Napoleon B. Smith. We also find that no blame whatsoever attaches to Mr. Smith, and wish to express our sympathy for him in what must be a matter of great personal regret and anxiety."

Period.

I stole a look at Napoleon B. The detective was completely relaxed, all the starch out of him.

"Thank you, gentlemen." Despite my antipathy to him, I found Dr. Bryce almost human when he smiled. "I can find absolutely no quarrel with your verdict, particularly as one who was so intimately connected with the entire unfortunate affair. We all trust that Mr. Smith will feel greatly relieved by the verdict of the jury, as I believe he has placed a good deal of unnecessary blame upon himself. I shall report your findings to the district attorney, gentlemen. You are now dismissed."

It was a very nice little speech, and I wanted to applaud. I could see, however, it was having no effect upon the large man.

I sidled up to him. "Let's go get some ice cream," I said. Napoleon B. turned the full look of ineffable sadness upon me. "No, thanks, Les." It was almost a sob. "It's very kind of you . . . but thanks just the same."

Then I knew he had it bad, and as the song says, that ain't good.

CHAPTER FOUR

At the time, I was busy writing the story of that famous Napoleon B. Smith mystery, *Crime at Cockcrow*, and I like to have my mind free when I am writing. Any outside disturbing element, when I am concentrating on a story, is liable to give me violent headaches that erupt in even more violent tempers disastrous to those around me.

With Napoleon B. Smith mooning around the house when he should have been securing evidence on a jewel theft, a missing heir, and some petty thievery from a restaurant chain, I fidgeted at my typewriter to the point where the page would still be blank after a half-hour of concentration. Finally, when I had reached the boiling point, I threw a handy manuscript at him. I was angry, anyway, because the manuscript had been rejected, and I thought of killing two birds with one stone. That manuscript stone damn near killed Napoleon B. It taught me something I had not known before, that the detective was vulnerable in the abdomen. At least, it doubled him up and caused him to moan. My feet took me out of the house, but fast.

When I returned some hours later, Napoleon B. greeted me with an apology rather than the left hook I expected.

It showed how far this preposterous obsession had downed him.

"I'm sorry, Les," he sighed, sagging all over his easy chair. "I know how hard it is for you to concentrate when an elephant like me is trying to make like a mouse, but I'm not myself these days."

"No," I snarled, still peeved, "you're two other guys, and I don't want to know either of them. I never thought a grown man could act the way you're acting."

"But you don't understand, Les; you don't understand at all. She was such a nice-looking old lady. She seemed so kind and gentle."

"And if she hadn't been woolly, she wouldn't have been down in that place." I became earnest because this was the first time the fat man had peeped to me in days about what was bothering him. "Look, she might have died at any time from old age, or from slipping on a banana peel, or . . . well, you name it. People that old die from anything and everything."

"But she didn't die from anything and everything," Napoleon B. explained patiently. "She died because I killed her."

"Rot!" I exploded. "You need a good, swift kick where it'll do you the most good!"

He agreed with me, with an air of utter melancholy.

"Aw nuts!" I said. "I'm getting out of here. I can't stand it any longer."

"Where you going, Les?"

"What's it to you? Anywhere to get away from this morgue." I couldn't help saying it, so I said it. "Maybe I'll even go play some golf."

As soon as I said it I was sorry, but a smile, fast-fading but a smile, fleeted across the great face.

"I asked for it and I got it, eh, Les? Going to Briar Hill?" That was rubbing it in.

"No," I answered hesitantly. "I thought of Oaklawn."

Now he grinned all over. "I was thinking of Briar Hill, myself. Want to come?"

When you've gone through the things I've gone through with Napoleon B. Smith you learn to expect almost anything and usually you get just that, but this was the strangest quick change of mind I'd ever known him to make. My jaw must have unhinged itself, for he gave a sudden explosive laugh.

"I don't want to play golf," he told me. "Put it down to what I've always said about criminals . . . that they return to the scene of the crime."

Too much is too much.

"You're crazy, Chief!" I almost yelled at him. "In your present state of mind . . . well, I give up!"

"It's just that I've been thinking."

"I know. That's the whole trouble with you. You've been sitting around for days turning things over in that lump of suet you call your mind, and now . . ."

"And now," he cut in with a still voice, "I've come up against some questions for which I can't find the answers."

That stopped me. "You mean . . ."

"I don't mean anything. I'd just like to get some peace of mind. I'd be able to sleep nights if I could prove my golf ball hadn't killed Mrs. Cartwright."

"Yeah, and I could make a million for a trip around the moon. Just forget about it, Napoleon B. Let yourself go and forget about it. You'll drive yourself batty, and me along with you."

"But . . ."

"You heard the evidence. It was an open-and-shut case—accidental death, very pure and very simple. Even you can't crack a nut like that to suit yourself."

The large man all but sneered at me. "That's what you said," he reminded me, "about at least a couple of dozen cases everybody else had given up."

"Yeah, but you had cases. There's no case in this."

Napoleon B. got up and wandered over to the Steinway. He balanced himself upon the piano stool and I held, my breath as I always did. Some day that piano stool is going to give up. His surprisingly long, hard fingers reached for the keys, and he began to ripple off the *Unfinished*, which was a concession to me, for it's my favorite piece of music.

"Then you run along and have your fun and games," he said above the music. "I'll . . . well, I'll just stay here."

The big baby!

"Oh, all right," I gave in. Schubert always crumples any resistance on my part. "I'll go get the clubs."

"I'm not playing—just looking."

He motioned me to a chair and paid me the supreme compliment of finishing the music to where Franz left off. You *have* to love a man like that.

Briar Hill slumbered in the sun. Napoleon B. had patiently caddied for me for the first six holes and I was beginning to feel like sixteen kinds of a heel. My score had been good, too; not par, but close. Then we came to the fateful seventh.

I knew my game would go all to pieces from here on in. As you've probably guessed by this time, I have more than a passing affection for that hulk of a man, nor am I in the least ashamed to admit it. I feel for him particularly when he's helpless and lost, like a child who's been scolded and expects a whipping at any moment. Maybe, as Napoleon B. says in his more cynical moments, it's the mother instinct in me.

Napoleon B. stood long on the tee of the seventh hole, looking towards the rough into which he had sliced. The dark blot in the shimmering sun was *Hell's Half-Acre*, and I shivered involuntarily at the sight of it.

After a while the large man said, quite placidly, "If you're the golfer you say you are, Les, you ought to be able to slice a ball into approximately the spot where I hit the other day, oughtn't you?"

He was serious; I could tell it. Without saying a word, I stepped up to the tee with my driver. To show how much I was feeling it, I teed up my favorite tournament ball. It's almost as hard for a good golfer to slice one off the tee as it is for a dub to hit one smack down the fairway, but what I did was turn towards the rough and drive that way. I knew I couldn't get Napoleon B's distance but I might have greater velocity and carrying power. It was a very nice two-seventy-five, even if I do say so myself.

"Not a bad imitation; not bad at all." It was almost a pleasure to hear the condescension return to the detective's voice. "Of course, mine was a longer drive, but . . ."

"But nothing!" I retorted. "I can't just deliberately step up to a tee and make a shot as bad as yours every day in the week."

Napoleon B. shook his huge head. "There!" he said to the landscape. "The man admits he's not as good as I am at making bad shots."

What can you do with a guy like that? All you can do is follow him, and hope for the best.

We walked along in the hot sunshine, not too quickly, for we were both inwardly reluctant to leave its bright shelter. It was the time of grasshoppers, and they made a very pleasant din in the orchestra of nature, a constant obbligato to the muted theme of the birds. In this pleasant setting it was hard to think of death.

Napoleon B. strode off down the fairway, angling off to the rough, with more purpose in his elephantine progress than I had seen in days. What's more, the big lout left the clubs for me to lug. I panted along behind him, doing my best to keep up.

"That ball of mine had quite a slice on it, as I seem to remember, Leslie." The words were jerky with his walking, but they seemed to be important to him. He rarely talked when he walked, one physical effort at a time being his usual limit.

"You can say that again!" I shot back.

He persisted, "More than that, there was quite a tail to it, wasn't there?"

"I never pay too much attention to your shots, but if it was like the usual it would have a tail a Chinese dragon need not be ashamed of. Why not ask the caddy? He'd remember better than I would. A bright kid. But I don't see, Chief, what . . ."

The goof kept on walking toward *Hell's Half-Acre*, not even looking back at me, ignoring the questions he knew to be in my mind. Maybe, I told myself, it's an early second childhood.

"It was a high shot, wasn't it?" he persisted.

"You had plenty of loft all right, but I don't see . . ."

He waggled his hand back at me impatiently. "Little man, you bother me. I'm asking the questions."

When he took that tone, I always let the starch out of me fast.

"How far," he went on, "would you say, speaking as the expert you think you are, it is from the tee to where my ball was found?"

I looked back a moment, then gazed ahead in concentration. Any good golfer can come close to distance.

"You want me to figure in slice and everything, Chief?"

"No, give it to me as the crow flies."

"I'd say pretty close to two-twenty-five. Not much more, anyway."

"Hmmmm. That's about what I thought myself. We'll have it measured exactly later. Now, counting slice and everything, I'd say that ball travelled three hundred yards. How's that?"

"That'd be about right. Could say three-twenty-five."

"Okay, my lad, keep those figures well in what you laughingly call your mind. Watch your step in the bad rough here. It's hard going for a little fellow like you."

Now that was what I called more like it! It's when Napoleon B. Smith goes formal on me and doesn't dig me with sharp cracks that I begin to worry about him. When he's needling me he's happy, and so am I.

We went scrambling through the undergrowth, down into the gloom of *Hell's Half-Acre*. I got back at him a bit by making a reference to the progress of a gazelle and an elephant, but Napoleon B. was much more like a lumbering bloodhound on the scent. I expected him to bay at any moment. It was a performance of which I never grew tired.

"Not much light gets in here," the fat man grumbled. "The old lady wasn't so far wrong in comparing it to Hudson's *Green Mansion*. I've seen jungles I prefer to this mess. I should have brought along a machete."

I told him it was all right, I had a flashlight.

"I said a *machete*, you dope, not a *match*. A machete is a sharp knife you cut your way through a jungle with."

As if I hadn't known it all the time.

We went more and more slowly down the path. It was an eerie feeling, traversing this thin path of tragedy, remembering what had gone before. Napoleon B. mumbled to himself as he went along. I caught odd words and phrases.

"Be badly trampled up . . . photographers . . . damned ambulance men . . . so-and-so police . . . lousy coroner . . . but maybe . . . maybe . . ."

Finally I spoke up. "Look here, Chief, what can you be expecting to find that hasn't already been found?"

For the first time he looked back at me. My flashlight was full in his face. This round object was all but obscured by what passed with him for an enigmatic smile.

"An easy conscience, perhaps," he said.

In a few moments we came to the spot. Already, rapid growth was beginning to obliterate what had been, after all, a very ordinary scene in an extraordinary setting. By some freak the sun slanted down through the tangled foliage to dapple the very place where the body had lain and make it comparatively light. I made inquisitive eyebrows at the large man.

"Have a good look around," he said expansively. "I've seen all I want to see."

"But you just got here," I protested. "How could you have seen *anything?*"

"That's because I'm smart," he grinned at me, "and you think I'm nuts. You know what they say about the thin line dividing genius and insanity."

"Are you hinting you're a genius?"

"Well, you wouldn't expect me to shout it, would you? A man has to observe certain proprieties. Well? What's the verdict, little man?"

"You should be confined to an institution for the rest of your unnatural life."

"I didn't mean that. I was talking about your feeling in regard to this place."

"If there's anything different, I can't see it."

The detective bent to straighten a delicate fern he had inadvertently caught with his heel. "No?"

"Well, it's grown up a bit, of course."

Napoleon B. stood erect again and gave me the look he reserved for the occasions when he considered me a moron. It combined exasperation and pity in nicely balanced quantities.

"I can't exactly blame you," he said. "It took me long enough to see it myself. In fact, we weren't meant to see it, and if it weren't for my streak of remorse, plus my infernal curiosity, we never would have."

"Let's have it straight," I demanded. "What are you driving at? What's going on here?"

"Nothing's *going* on, infant. Something's *gone* on."

"Oh, for Pete's sake, what?"

He timed it very nicely. There was the proper dramatic pause before he said:

"Murder!"

CHAPTER FIVE

When a man stands there. and throws the word "murder" at you, it takes a few seconds for your mind to adjust itself to all the implications. But when that man is Napoleon B. Smith, a famous detective, looking for an out for something that should never have given him a sleepless hour in the first place, it is hard to refrain from doing exactly what I did.

I laughed.

"'Murder,' he says!" I guffawed again. "Now look, Napoleon B., I've humored you long enough in this, and . . ."

He cut in on me with a misquotation, given placidly, which was proof he felt himself on solid ground. "'There's none so blind as those who will not see.'"

"Nor none so dumb as those who won't give up when they know they're licked, either."

"All right, smarty." He made me uneasy the way he kept his temper. "You look around again and tell me what you *don't* see."

I tried, but it was no use.

"Then tell me," he went on in his gentle voice, "do you see any way a dropping golf ball could hit anyone hard enough to kill?"

There it was. It was so plain, it shrieked after you saw it.

"Wait a minute!" I yelled. "A golf ball . . . this place . . . why, it's impossible! The whole thing's leafed over as thickly as any jungle!"

Napoleon B. turned on a full-sized sunrise.

"Okay, Les," he beamed, "now you're getting on the beam. We've talked about this place so much as old Mrs. Cartwright's *Green Mansions* that we couldn't see the jungle for the trees. No golf ball could ever drop through this entanglement with sufficient force to make a bruise, much less to kill anyone, even an old lady with heart trouble. Why, to drop anything in here might even force the repeal of Newton's law of gravity."

I'd been looking around with more interest, my mind jumping from island to island of new possibilities.

"How about a ricochet shot from one tree to another?" I asked, but it was more a formality than anything. I didn't need Napoleon B's shake of the head to convince me it was an impossibility where trees grew so close together they looked like a crowd in a New York subway.

"Anyway," clinched the detective, "I've always noticed that ricochet shots come on low, hard-driven balls."

"I'm away ahead of you," I said. "The best tournament ball in the world couldn't bounce through this underbrush. In fact, it's enough to stop a jeep."

"Besides, we've agreed mine was a high shot. You've been standing well down the fairway when somebody's got off a pretty fair drive with a lot of loft on it. Does a ball roll or bounce much when it's hit like that?"

"You win again, Napoleon B. Any shot like that lands with a dull thud, and rolls only a few feet. But what's all this getting to?"

"It's getting to a golf ball that travelled too slowly to have killed an old lady. It's adding up to a wrong verdict by a coroner's jury."

It was airtight, and it was good news. Reopen the inquest with the new evidence, clear Napoleon B. Smith, and he and I can get back to normal living again.

"But you said *murder*," I prompted him.

"I can dream, can't I?" The fat man was his old expansive self. "Les, this calls for a celebration. Two . . . no, make it three . . . dishes of ice cream."

"I'll treat," I answered mechanically. It was always expected of me in moments of jubilation like this. "But why murder?"

"Well, why not?"

"It could be heart failure . . ."

"And she could have been struck over the head with a tiddlywink. How about the bruise?"

"Bruise?"

"Where's that memory you're always bragging about?"

"Oh, *that*."

"Sure, *that*."

I began to think about the old lady and her queerness, and I began to think, too, about Napoleon B. Smith and his queerness, and I felt dizzy. So I gave up, and played along with the fat man.

"All right," I babied, "what's the first move in your desire to rehabilitate yourself?"

The detective was too happy to respond in kind. "I'm not concerned with myself any longer. As long as I'm convinced in my own mind that it wasn't my fault, then it doesn't matter what anyone else thinks. But I've been put to a strain, my boy." A shadow waltzed across a suddenly sober face. "I have a feeling that I've not only made a fool of myself but that somebody's made a fool of me. That can't be, Les, that can't be."

"You mean you've had your ego stepped on?"

"Put it that way if you want to," he smiled, "and you obviously want to. No, tender comrade, I am now upon the scent for Justice. My professional instincts are aroused. At any moment . . ."

". . . I can expect you to bay," I put in. "All right, cut the red tape. What gives?"

"We apply to Dr. Bryce for an order for exhumation upon the strength of new evidence. If an autopsy proves death was due to natural causes, well, nobody's been hurt. If, on the other hand, there's been what you newspapermen call foul play . . ." He winked at me. ". . . I smell a nice, fat fee," he finished.

That's always okay by me.

Dr. Bryce was almost cordial for him, but I was beginning to suspect his bark was worse than his bite. He heard Napoleon B. Smith's story with only an odd exclamation or two. When the fat man finished, the coroner screwed up his lips into a thin smile.

"You know, Napoleon B.," he said, "that's ingenious. Even for you, it's ingenious."

The detective snorted. "Even for me or anybody, Doctor. Ask Les here. He saw it, too."

Bryce gave me a nasty once-over. "Ah, yes, the sleepy Mr. Allen. Well?"

"It's just like Napoleon B. says, Doc," I answered, knowing it would make him angry, and not liking his crack any too well myself. "A golf ball dropping down into that mess wouldn't have enough oomph left to swat a fly."

The telephone rang. When the doctor answered I could tell he didn't want to talk to whomever it was in front of us. But we just sat there, and he ended the one-sided conversation by saying that he couldn't tell anything from symptoms over the phone and that he'd have to make a personal diagnosis. After he hung up he was his old, snappish self.

"It's an impossibility, Napoleon B.," he said. "An utter impossibility. You know as well as I do that I could not order the inquest reopened unless there was a definite suspicion of foul play, something you certainly have not proved to me. As for an order for exhumation, that's hardly my province. It's up to the district attorney or the relatives. You haven't given the district attorney anything to go on that I can see. From what I know of the old lady's relatives, there isn't a chance there, either."

Napoleon B. was grim. "Look, Tom Bryce; you know me. We've been through these things before. I wouldn't ask for anything where I didn't think there was more than a fifty-fifty chance of success. You take a chance on ordering an exhumation, and I'll see you get most of the credit."

This was a painful offer for the large man and the coroner knew it. If there was one thing Napoleon B. liked, next to ice cream, it was the limelight . . . as long as it was favorable. But Dr. Bryce shook his precise head.

"I'd like to," he said. "I'm reluctant not to, but . . ."

"You won't?"

"That's right. You know the law as well as I do, Napoleon B., perhaps better. Perhaps I could stretch a point. Maybe I should do it for the sake of our harmonious relationship. But, frankly, I can see no reason for doing so. If you'll pardon me, your vanity throughout this entire matter has been a trifle absurd. Most other men would have accepted the just verdict of the jury, and been satisfied."

"But I'm not most other men," said the detective so quietly I knew he was furiously angry. "I'm Napoleon B. Smith. I'm a detective. In case you've forgotten, I get results."

He got up with more dignity than was usual with him, and ambled to the door. I followed behind impatiently; I definitely didn't like Dr. Bryce in the first place, and I was violently opposed to anyone who hurt the fat man, as Napoleon B. was obviously hurt. With his hand on the door knob, the detective turned and faced the coroner.

"That's one thing you'll recall about me from your previous experiences," he said. "*I get results.*"

You've got to admit it was a nice exit line.

CHAPTER SIX

That was only the beginning.

Our next stop was at the office of Adam Johnson, the Cartwright's lawyer. He was reputed to be one of the wealthiest attorneys in town, but his offices were dingy and badly lighted, smelling of old law books, and cheap whiskey, to both of which Johnson was addicted. He was so stuffy he even employed a male secretary, a prissy soul who would have been an old maid had he worn skirts. Sometimes I suspected him of a girdle.

Johnson unjackknifed himself when his secretary had shown us the way in with as much ceremony as though we had not been in the office a half a hundred times before. His jagged teeth split his lips in a wolfish smile.

"Come in! Come in!" he called affably enough, and motioned us to two of his moth-eaten black leather chairs. I got the one where the spring drove into the spine at just the right point to make you wish you were elsewhere. "Cigar?"

Napoleon B. waved the stogie away, but I never did have the heart to refuse anything free. I was sorry for it afterwards, because what this country still needs is a good five-cent cigar.

"What's on your mind, Napoleon B.?" asked the lawyer, opening on a conventional gambit.

"Nothing that a little cooperation from you won't cure, Adam. It's this Cartwright affair."

The lawyer made a deprecatory gesture with one of his long, bony hands. "Too bad about that, Napoleon B. I've heard you were pretty upset about it. No need to be, you know."

"Absolutely none," said the fat man placidly.

Johnson's eyes sharpened, but he was smart enough to wait for Napoleon B. to go on. A cagey customer, Johnson.

I shifted in my chair to get a better look at Napoleon B. He was gazing dreamily out the window. Two cagey customers in one room was too much. I had to say something. I said, "Napoleon's got a B. in his bonnet."

It wasn't a very good gag.

"You're the Cartwright lawyer, aren't you, Adam?" the detective asked of the open window.

"Yes," Johnson replied to his shabbily bound Blackstone.

Napoleon B. moved his queen boldly. "I want an order for the exhumation of the body of Mrs. Cartwright," he said abruptly.

That got Johnson for a moment. He'd probably figured out every move on the board but that one.

"W . . . what!" he stuttered.

The detective repeated his request. This time Johnson laughed, a harsh and unconvinced laugh, a puzzled laugh.

"I don't get it," Johnson said finally. "You've been so tough on so many cases, Napoleon B. We've fought each other to a standstill several times. Yet you've let an accidental death get you so stewed up you're going around making batty requests like an order for an exhumation."

"It's not a batty request." Napoleon B. had found something of interest in the Golden Nugget Tea Room sign across the street. "It's a perfectly logical idea. I'm on to something."

Johnson thought that over, then asked what.

"I don't know. Just something. I know I didn't kill the old lady anyway, nor did my golf ball."

"A coroner's jury says you did."

"Didn't you ever know a jury to be wrong?" The eyes twinkled in the large face, and Johnson bared his fangs appreciatively. "That golf ball of mine couldn't have killed her. Ask Les."

I picked up my cue smartly and said, no, it couldn't.

Then, because Napoleon B. gave me a little nod, I told why it couldn't have.

"It seems like a mountain out of a molehill, Napoleon B.," said Johnson. "All along, it's seemed like that. I don't understand you."

"Maybe I'm just stubborn. Can you get me the order?"

Johnson shrugged his narrow shoulders. "On what evidence? You know the family would never consent. You'd have to get the consent of one of the family, and you'd never get it."

The thrust went home, and Johnson twiddled it around a bit with a sneer.

"Oh, I see." Napoleon B. was now looking directly at the lawyer, a sign of imminent defeat. "Why?"

"Why? Well, think it over for yourself. If you were asked for an exhumation of your mother's corpse . . . by the way, you had a mother, didn't you?"

Napoleon B. picked himself up with considerable dignity. "Yeah. I knew *mine*." He beckoned me with his eyes, and we went out.

"You give in easy," I said, outside.

The hand he clapped on my shoulder may have seemed friendly to anyone passing by, but I bruise easily and Napoleon B. knows it.

"There's an ice-cream parlor across the street," he told me, applying the pressure. "How about it?"

I couldn't really say no because he was steering me to the place in question with that one big paw on my shoulder It was one of those old-fashioned parlors, with wire-backed seats. We took the table nearest the window. I couldn't help noticing it gave us a full view of Johnson's office and entrance. Napoleon B. ordered a banana royal, with a side dish of marshmallow sundae. When I ordered a coke the large man took his eyes from Johnson's office long enough to wither me for my plebian tastes.

Napoleon B. was halfway through the marshmallow sundae, and complaining about the stinginess of the proprietor with his ice-cream scoop when he abruptly put down his spoon and told me to follow him. Remembering my aching shoulder and realizing that only something of importance could make him leave his unfinished dish, I went along more or less willingly. My interest quickened immediately when I saw that what interested Napoleon B. was a well-turned ankle vanishing up the stairway to Johnson's office. It interested me, too.

The detective practically sprinted across the street. I heard him heaving himself creakingly up the stairs and I caught up to him just as he was stage-whispering, "Miss Cartwright." The well-turned ankle turned well, and it was possessed by the frigid vision of the inquest, Gale Cartwright. She was positively arctic when she saw who had called her.

"I beg your pardon!" What she really meant was, "You've got a hell of a nerve!"

Napoleon B. went on unabashedly, "Please, Miss Cartwright, if you will, I'd like to talk to you for a moment. It's very important to me, very important."

Something about his earnestness must have impressed the girl because she nodded slowly, as though convincing herself, and came down the stairs. Just when I was thinking she was human, she caught sight of me and the thaw stopped. But Napoleon B's hand was now on her arm, and I've already explained about that.

We made our way back to the ice-cream shop. The proprietor was clearing our table. The fat man let out a bellow that must have made the poor Italian think the Mafia had arrived. He dropped the dishes with a clatter. Napoleon. B. was furious.

"Damned robber!" he swore. "A man can't turn his back but what you make off with his last dish of ice cream. Now look what you've done! Get me more ice cream to make up for what you've lost, do you hear?"

The proprietor was going into some furious expostulations, but I winked at him and waved a two-dollar bill where Napoleon B. couldn't see it. It was a magic poultice. Instantly, he became humble and contrite, apologizing all over the place to the detective in Italian that popgunned without making a dent. Napoleon B., somewhat mollified by the man's obviously conciliatory gestures, seated his vast hulk daintily on the wire chair, while it groaned in protest.

I heard a tinkle of laughter. Turning, I looked full at Miss Cartwright. She returned my gaze frankly. There was, I told myself, a bond. The lady had her points, and her curves, too.

Napoleon B., after seating himself, had picked up one of the long spoons in anticipation. He saw me and gestured the spoon at Miss Cartwright. "Young lady," he said, with his often elephantine humor, "that young man is not a character from *Red Riding Hood*, but his eyes are the better to see you with, and his teeth are . . ."

Miss Cartwright now laughed frankly and freely and sat down. "Aren't you going to ask me to have a banana split, Mr. Smith?" she dimpled.

Napoleon B. raised an eyebrow at me. "*He* squires all the young ladies." Once again the spoon waved. "Ask him. But won't it be bad for your figure?"

Nothing could be bad for that figure, my eyes said.

"Put 'em back in your head," said the large man, "and go tell Mussolini the lady's splitting a banana with us."

I hope my back showed him what I thought of his rudeness. But he did not seem to be paying me much attention when I returned from giving my order to Garibaldi. In fact, he was talking with some animation.

". . . and I know I haven't any right to expect it, Miss Cartwright, but I'm hoping to enlist your sympathy," he was saying.

"I loved my stepmother." Her voice was low and throaty, giving me little shivers.

"I'm sure you did. That's what makes it so very hard." He saw the ice cream coming. "You'll pardon me if I break off here. I never allow business to interfere with my one pleasure. Les will probably be glad to entertain you with sheep's eyes."

I was indignant. "You just said I was a wolf," I told him. "How can I have sheep's eyes?"

He spooned up a large mess of goo. "Because you're wolf in sheep's eyes clothing," he remarked placidly, and fed himself, dribbling a bit.

I was utterly crushed, especially as Miss Cartwright laughed more heartily than ever at my discomfit. But, while Napoleon B. ate with religious fervor and the girl dug at her banana split as though waistlines were no concern of hers, I improved my time. I flattered myself that, before the detective licked the last spoonful regretfully, I had the pole position with that filly.

"Miss Cartwright," Napoleon B. cut into one of my best wisecracks abruptly, "what do you think of me?"

She hesitated. "Why . . . why, I'm quite an admirer of yours, Mr. Smith. I've read every book about you that Mr. Allen has ever written."

That bucked me.

"And you still admire me?" The fat man licked an ice-creamed finger delicately. "Wonderful fortitude! Marvelous stamina! What I mean is, do you think, after what's happened, that I'm to be trusted?"

"It was an accident, Mr. Smith," she protested. "I tried, but I couldn't hold it against you. It might have happened to anyone."

"Suppose it wasn't an accident?"

Her face showed undiluted surprise. "I *beg* your pardon? It's hardly a matter for joking!"

He wagged a fat forefinger at her indulgently. "And I'm not joking, miss. I have reason to believe . . . no, I'm *certain* that your stepmother was not killed by my golf ball. I have further reason to believe that she did not meet her death naturally, and my reasoning is this: if I did not kill her, someone expected her to be found and her death attributed to natural causes. Fate brought me into the affair unexpectedly . . . the chance lie of my golf ball . . . the bruise on the head. Ah, but that is what you must remember, miss—the bruise on the head! Was it more than a bruise? The doctor examined her only superficially because it appeared patent at the time that my golf ball had killed her. Now, that theory is absurd; I have evidence to that effect. But the bruise remains. What caused the bruise? It could not have been from a fall if she died of heart failure. Your stepmother lay on her back. I repeat: what caused the bruise?"

She struggled for words, then finally said banally "What?"

"That's what I'd like to know. And you can help me."

"I?"

His finger now speared her. "Miss Cartwright, why were you going to Johnson's office just now?"

"Why . . . why, he sent for me."

"Sent for you?"

"To hear the will read."

"Ah!" It was an expelled breath; rather than an exclamation. "That's what I thought. I knew the old fox had something up his sleeve besides that bone he calls an arm. Miss Cartwright, I want to be your representative!"

I was getting dizzier by the sentence. So was Miss Lovely. She drew her summer furs about her indecisively, the way women do when they are trying to distract your attention, or simply to distract you. But Napoleon B. rushed on, treading on the angel. "I want to represent you legally at the reading of the will. Miss Cartwright, if you could do something for the memory of your stepmother, would you?"

"Anything!"

Her back was to the window, but I could see why the detective was hurrying. The other members of the Cartwright clan had disappeared up the stairs to the lawyer's office in the past ten minutes.

"Then let me represent you at the reading of the will." He waggled a fat finger at me. "With my secretary here, of course."

"Huh?" I exploded, but he gave me a keep-quiet signal.

"But where does that help my stepmother, Mr. Smith?"

"You'll have to trust me, my dear." His fat grin was fatuous. "I'm quite trustworthy, you know."

Yeah, I jeered mentally, and so is a rattlesnake if you let it sleep.

The girl came to a decision. "I don't know why, Mr. Smith, but I'll do it! It isn't rational, yet I am going on your reputation."

Napoleon B. practically took a bow on that one. "Johnson'll try to throw us out," he warned. "It will be up to you to stand firm."

All he had to do was look at that chin. I was looking at it, and other things, too.

CHAPTER SEVEN

Johnson's prissy secretary nearly had conniptions when we walked in. Between trying to bow to Gale Cartwright and shoot furious glances at us, he was in a bad way.

"Good day, Miss Cartwright, good day, lovely day," he fussed. "Go right in, they're waiting for you." He attempted to bar us from following. "You can't go in there, gentlemen, you simply *can't!* Mr. Johnson will be *furious!*"

Napoleon B. put a hand on the poor little guy's shoulder. I winced with him. An invisible force propelled the secretary out of our way. Miss Cartwright swept into Johnson's dingy office with a flounce of furs, while I followed her worshipfully and the detective came in through the narrow door sidewise. Johnson half-rose out of his swivel chair when he saw us.

"What's the meaning of this?" he barked. "You know very well this is a family conference, Miss Cartwright."

"Mr. Smith is my representative," said Gale grandly.

"Mr. Allen is my secretary," contributed Napoleon B.

"This is a highly irregular procedure, Mr. Smith." Johnson looked more like a bald-headed eagle than ever, and his

feathers were ruffled. "It is quite permissible for Miss Cartwright to remain, but I must ask you and your . . . uh . . .
secretary to leave."

A deep, quiet voice from the shadows near the bookcase
said, "Oh, let them stay, Johnson. It'll be public property
tomorrow. Why make a mountain out of a molehill?"

It was handsome Cyrus Handley, the skeet shot, speaking. The girl flashed him a grateful smile that wasn't lost on
him any more than it was on me.

"Yeah, what difference can it make?" The way Jack Cartwright said it, it was an insult. He was slouched down in the
chair with the broken spring. I knew he had no spine for it
to rub against.

"Very well," the lawyer reluctantly consented. "I suppose you all know what you're doing. But this man Smith
is tricky. I wouldn't trust him as far as I could throw him."

Cyrus Handley laughed at that. It was funny when you
thought of it; skinny Johnson couldn't have budged the fat
man an inch. But I liked Handley for his laughter.

Johnson, offended, picked up the papers in front of him.
I noticed his hands were rattling the papers, presumably
from hidden anger. In a harsh voice he proceeded to read
the last will and testament of the old lady whom I had never
known in life but met in death.

It was a long-winded affair and boring to me, if not to
three persons in that room. Boiled down, it said this:

> John Cartwright, the stepson; property, bonds,
>   and cash amounting to some seven million
>   dollars.
> Cyrus Handley, her nephew; some four million
>   dollars.

> The balance to charities, amounting to about
> another million, with the exception of a be-
> quest to her stepdaughter, Gale Cartwright,
> of one hundred thousand dollars, "for her
> faithful services, and for her many kind-
> nesses to me in all but the one important
> instance of which she will be fully aware."

A tiny handkerchief flew to Gale Cartwright's eyes at these words from the dead, and I saw that Napoleon B. looked startled and upset. As Gale sobbed, and before I could move, Handley crossed over to her and laid a kindly hand on her arm.

"It's too bad, Gale," he said, and in the silence his low voice was loud. "I'm sure your mother didn't mean it just the way it sounds."

"I'm glad you understand, Cy," the girl answered between sobs. "It . . . it isn't the money . . . it's what Mother said. How . . . how *could* she?"

"Not much it isn't the money!" It was a sneer from Jack Cartwright. "Anybody who likes money the way you do can't sit there and tell me that you . . ."

"Shut up!"

The way Cyrus Handley said it made me shiver. It stopped Cartwright with his mean mouth half-open. He snapped it shut on a word he would never say. But there was murder in the look he gave Handley.

Johnson cleared his throat uneasily. "I trust there will be no unpleasant feelings." His tone poured gasoline on the fire. "Wills are . . . well, wills are very capricious things. I remember the case of Jamieson, pere. He was . . ."

Nobody was listening.

"Take me home, please, Cy," said Gale faintly.

He supported her from the room. Have I remarked how utterly charming she looked in black?

Unexpectedly, Jack Cartwright began to blubber, "That's the way! You all see how it is. That's the way my own sister treats me. She hates me! Everybody hates me! I wish I were dead!"

So did we.

"I think," said Napoleon B. pointedly to Johnson, who was decidedly uncomfortable, "that this calls for a celebration. Don't you agree, Adam?"

The lawyer took the hint. He brought out a squat bottle from his desk and four dirty looking tumblers. He pressed a buzzer and old percy-pants came in. Johnson ordered water, but apparently it was for a chaser, not to wash the glasses. I hoped that whiskey was a good disinfectant.

Napoleon B. segued from *Stormy Weather* into *St. Louis Blues*. He always claimed that blues music was the best "concentrator" he knew. I know it kept me from my writing, even with earplugs. All I could do was grin, even if I couldn't bear it.

As his long fingers rippled over the keys gracefully, and the piano stool teetered like crazy, he said, presumably to me, "I wonder what the old lady meant saying 'in all but the one important instance of which she will be fully aware'?"

It was a rhetorical question. I kept mum.

"Evidently the girl took it pretty hard." He hated to see the evening sun go down for a third chorus. "She seems somewhat sweet on her stepcousin."

"Yeah," I admitted sourly. The same thing had been bothering me. "Say, what was all that *representative* gag about? You could have read about the will in the papers."

He began to out-boogie Maurice Rocco.

"And miss all the fun?" he asked complacently. "Besides, Miss Cartwright needs a representative. Has it ever occurred to you that Miss Cartwright requires looking after?"

I said it had.

"I don't mean that way, dope. Up until this afternoon's session at Johnson's I wouldn't have given a zloty for her chances of survival. Now, I don't know what to think."

This was news, indeed! The big ape had stumbled onto something, and apparently stumbled off it, too.

"What's up?" I demanded.

"Just a little intuition."

"Oh, *that!*"

Now he was playing *Basin Street Blues*, and my toes were tapping in spite of me.

"Don't sneer at my clairvoyance, little man," he said. "It's been useful many times. For instance, in the case of golf balls that don't kill. But there's something very screwy in Somaliland about this whole setup. I must get an exhumation order." His fingers came off the piano keys in the middle of a bar. "Get dressed! We're going out."

I was sitting around in my underwear and an old pair of shorts. At the moment, I could think of a dozen things that I would rather do than disturb myself, but when Napoleon B. Smith speaks to you like that, your muscles start moving before your brain.

We drove recklessly; that is to say, Napoleon B. Smith fancied himself better than Jehu, on or off the track, and always proceeded with an abandon that took years off my life. The detective was a driver who proceeded on the theory that everything, including houses and trees, should make way for an oncoming automobile. To put it succinctly, he

drove an automobile as he played golf. It was with a feeling
of relief on my part and satisfaction on his that we finally
screeched to a stop before the snooty Worthington Palace
Arms.

"Gingerbread!" snorted Napoleon B., waving aside a gilt-
and-blue doorman who stood under the affected canopy
and sought to inquire our business. "Damn poor architecture! Outrageous snobbery! Harrumph!"

The last was for the doorman who, recognizing vaguely
that here was an innate authority to match his own assumed
airs, stepped to one side, his attitude saying plainly that
the world was full of people and they all bothered him. We
proceeded up the red plush carpet to the hideous red-and-
cream elevator.

"Comes the revolution," said Napoleon B. darkly, "I shall
order all such apartment houses turned into nurseries." The
detective was always leading an imaginary revolt. "Third
floor," he added to the supercilious elevator operator, "and
make it snappy!"

I wondered where we were going, but knew better than
to ask. Napoleon B. had taken only a lightning glance at the
tenants' directory as we passed it in the hall, but he always
saw more in a quick look than most men in a full scrutiny.

The attendant slammed the doors behind us, obviously
put out by being addressed so uncouthly by men who were
not gentlemen. The hall was deep in wine carpet. Even the
large man's heavy footsteps made no sound.

The door we stopped before was "309"; the name on the
card, "John Cartwright." Napoleon B. was about to punch
the buzzer when he held up his finger. A voice, loud and
sneering, was coming through the thick panels. There was
no mistaking the owner of the voice.

"I don't give a damn for 'em!" Jack Cartwright was drunk as usual. "I don't give a damn for you! I don't give a damn f'anybody!"

Somebody said something soothing in low and indistinguishable tones. It was impossible to tell whether it was a man or a woman. I was about to say something myself when the detective motioned me furiously to silence.

"Seven million bucks . . . and 's'all mine! If you think I'm goin' share it with you, you're crazy!" Here he burped very loudly. "Let's have 'nudder l'il drink, huh, jus' pledge our friendship?"

There were more mumbles.

"Aw, *that* big, fat slob! Who's afraid of him, huh, who's 'fraid him? Not me, tha's not who." Ice tinkled in a glass, and soda was siphoned. "Well, here's to crime!" More whispers. "I will not shuddup. Not for you, nor anybody else. Once is 'nough in one day . . . once is too much, d'yuh hear? You gotta be careful with what *I* know." Cartwright chortled horribly. "Don't worry 'bout that fat shlob detective, I tell yuh. He isn't on to a thing . . . not a thing . . . 'less I tell him."

The unknown voice spoke again, almost inaudibly.

"I will *not!*" Cartwright's words were almost shrieked. "Never gave nothin' 'way in my life, 'specially murder. Don't know nothin'. Never say nothin'."

Napoleon B. was probably thinking what I was thinking: of all the luck! I saw his air of triumph as he put his shoulder to the door for a preliminary test.

"Can hold my liquor. Can always hold my liquor. Shhh! Never say a word. Tha's me. Shhhh!" I could all but see the drunken fool with his finger to his lips. "Won' say a word." Suddenly there was drunken alarm. "Here! Watcha doin'?

Get 'way from that drawer! That's *my* gun. Put it down!
Don't! Don't shoot!"

His thin, foolish scream was drowned in the report of
the gun and the thunder of Napoleon B's shoulder against
the stout oak. The door creaked, but held.

"Stand back!" yelled the detective, grabbing for his
shoulder holster.

Two quick shots from his police revolver blew out the
lock. The door swung in.

I registered these things almost at once:

> Jack Cartwright, his face horribly contorted
> with his last drunken fear, had half the top
> of his head blown off, and there was still a
> twitch in the legs.
> A revolver, smoke coming from its mouth, lay
> on the table.
> A handkerchief was on the floor near the table,
> a woman's handkerchief.
> The swinging door leading to the rear of the
> apartment was just stopping its motion.

Napoleon B. streaked for that door, gun in hand.

I got down on my hands and knees to look at the handkerchief. Yes, I *had* seen it before, that very afternoon, as a
matter of fact.

I stared, fascinated, at the initials, "G. C."

Then I put the handkerchief in my pocket.

CHAPTER EIGHT

Inspector Joe Brownlee was boiling. Looked at from his point of view, you could scarcely blame him. He had started on the beat with Napoleon B. and had no fear whatsoever of the large man.

"So you have to play the big hero and blast holes in locked doors," he said so sarcastically Napoleon B's big ears reddened. "You didn't think you'd wake the dead that way, did you? And you certainly managed to scare the living."

"I couldn't have been thirty seconds behind the murderer." The detective was on the defensive, and I grinned within myself. "How'd *I* know the kitchen door was going to be so small I'd get stuck?"

Brownlee turned away from him with a snort. "Ever look at yourself in the mirror?" he jerked over his shoulder, and knelt beside the body. "Got everything, Bert? Jim?"

The photographer and the fingerprint man nodded. The latter made some rather acrid comment about meddling private dicks who didn't know enough not to grab door knobs, but Brownlee made no comment. He knew that once we shot the lock off we had to get in that door fast. The fingerprint joe also mentioned that there seemed to be very few clear prints in the apartment, indicating whoever had been here had worn gloves. At least that was his guess; he'd verify it later, he said, as he took prints from the stiff, a difficult process.

While he was talking, Dr. Bryce bustled in. He took one horrified look. "My God!" he said. "Not another Cartwright!"

He seemed very shaken, but he went right to work. In a few minutes he put his gloves back on and pulled a sheet over the mess. Brownlee, in the meantime, had been looking around the paneling, called over the photographer, had a shot made of a hole in the wall, then took his jackknife and dug out a bullet. He put the bullet carefully in his handkerchief. I could see Napoleon B. making plenty of mental notes. He knew that Brownlee worked well and with a minimum loss of time, which is all to the good in the police business.

Of course, the entire Worthington Palace Arms had long since turned itself inside out with excitement. The doorman had appeared, given us the o. o. as though we were already convicted and sentenced to be hanged, and had departed with his visor at a forty-five-degree angle of superiority when barked at by Joe Brownlee. Various and sundry females and males in assortments of attire had paraded to the shattered door, had asked the inevitable questions and had then departed, after leaving names with a bored police officer. It would be a long time before the Worthington Palace Arms would live down its free publicity of a front-page murder. It was now on a par with the Globe Hotel, two blocks down, and Barney's Flop, the other side of town. The face was the same but the attitude would have to be more human.

Inspector Brownlee was just about ready to call it a night and leave two men on guard, front and rear, when somebody was heard trying the back door. We all froze to instant silence. The cops unlimbered their artillery and waited. The intruder hummed a little song in the passageway, pushed open the door.

"Stand where you are! You're covered!" shouted the Inspector.

The man in the doorway fainted.

When they brought him around he said his name was Marcel Leblanc, he was the personal servant of Monsieur Cartwright, he had been having the evening off, and why should they frighten the living daylights out of him?

Brownlee silently drew back the sheet about two feet. Leblanc let out a shriek, but did not collapse this time.

"'Oo deed thees?" he demanded.

"Now, *there's* a $64 question," Brownlee snorted. "Where've you been all evening?"

"Monsieur Cartwright, 'e tell me to go hout. I go hout. I go hout to cinema."

"Where?"

Napoleon B. explained mildly that the man only meant the movies.

"Then why the hell doesn't he say so? Okay, we can check on that later. Why'd your boss tell you to go out?"

"'E deedn' say. 'E joos' say go hout. 'E do that many time w'en he desire to be alone avec les femmes."

"Huh?"

"When he wants to smoosh with dames," I cut in inelegantly.

Brownlee gave me a dirty look. "*That* you'd know all about, Allen. Look here, Frenchy, don't you know what dame, I mean, woman was coming here?"

Marcel drew himself up to his full five feet, four-and-ahalf inches. "I," he said with great dignity, "do not make the enquiries into my master's affaires de coeur."

Brownlee looked him over with new respect. "Yeah, the guy was a rat from all accounts," he agreed. "Affairs de cur . . . so that's what you call 'em, eh?" He laughed shortly. "You Frenchies always have a word for everything. Well, I guess . . ."

"Do you mind, Joe?" cut in Napoleon B. smoothly.

The Inspector waved a disgusted hand.

"Marcel!"

The valet stiffened. Here was a new voice, and the accent was good, too. "Oui, monsieur?"

I can follow some French conversations, but not that one. Napoleon B. talked with his hands more than Marcel Leblanc. But one word, repeated twice, made me shiver. The valet referred twice to "Gale." The conversation was all over before Brownlee awoke to his official dignity.

"You shouldn't ought've done that, Napoleon B.," he complained. "You know it's against regulations. What'd the guy say, anyway?"

"He said he knows nothin' from nothin'," said Napoleon B. blandly, and gave me the shut-up signal.

Brownlee told Leblanc to hold himself in readiness for questions at any time and not to leave the city. He could stay at the apartment if he wished, to which the valet shook an emphatic negative.

"As for you guys," the Inspector said to us, "for gawdsake don't go messin' into things. I got enough troubles as it is." Then he added inconsistently, "Don't forget to keep me posted, Napoleon B., if you snag onto anything."

The large man ducked around a big truck, skidded by a streetcar, and beat a red light. I could see he was preoccupied.

"If you have no respect for the city ordinances," I told him with acid, "at least pause to think of the financial conditions of our insurance companies."

His reply was to take one paw off the wheel and hold it out to me. "Gimme!" he said with admirable terseness.

I played innocent.

"Hand it over!" When Napoleon B. used that tone he never failed to get obedience. It was what I called his "killer" voice. "I've got eyes in my head, haven't I?"

Now, I ask you, they must be in the back of his head, mustn't they? It took him about three seconds to cross that apartment, but I have no doubt he had inventoried everything in it while sashaying after the murderer. In those few seconds of time his fast-clicking brain could register everything around him, no matter what he was intent upon. I remember once quizzing him about it because the trick fascinated me. But, like most tricks, it had a simple explanation. It was a professional extension of the familiar Boy Scout observation test carried to the nth degree; you know, the test where you are given a number of objects, given a minute to mentally catalogue them, and then asked to name them. As you proceed in the test you can multiply the number of objects or cut down the time, even with but a normal memory. And the large detective had a truly photographic mind; his head was so crammed with seemingly irrelevant facts that I often wondered how it had room for anything else.

Because I knew that he had seen the handkerchief and had only been wistfully hoping that he had not, I gave him the wispy thing. It disappeared into his big hand as though it had never existed. The light was against us so for once he stopped, almost knocking my head against the windshield in the process. He tried to examine the handkerchief but it was too dark.

"Switch on the dome fight," he said, then sniffed at the small linen square with its lace border.

I was about to comply when he stopped me.

"Never mind, Les. I know who owned it. It's *Nuit de Joie*, and only the filthy rich can afford it, and I smelt it this afternoon in Johnson's office when Miss Cartwright held it to her dainty nose."

It was obvious what he was thinking. She could also have held it to wipe fingerprints from a gun if she had not been wearing gloves, and could have then dropped the incriminating evidence in her excitement.

"Lots of people use this *Nuit de Joie*," I defended.

"I can easily prove it by looking at the initials I feel under my fingers." The cars behind honked impatiently and Napoleon B. started away with a jerk that threw my head violently back against the upholstery. It's a mystery to me why I am never prepared for his driving. "Want to stop under this street light?"

"Never mind," I acknowledged defeat. "The initials are G. C., you assorted species of bloodhound."

He was extraordinarily gentle when he spoke again. "You're an incurable romantic, Les. It does your sensibilities credit, but it also indicates softening of the brain. When will you ever learn that a pretty face and a neat ankle do not necessarily indicate heavenly attributes?"

"Never, I guess," I confessed, "but you must admit they sure help."

"They have helped you on the downward path, my boy." When he becomes excessively paternal, I know he is worried about me or about something I've done. "I suppose you know you've compounded felony."

"Who's to know?"

"I do. And if this case continues on its present trend, I may be forced to tell Inspector Brownlee." He would, too. "I wouldn't like to, but it's a matter of duty. Whatever made you do such a fool thing?"

"I suppose I'm just too impulsive!"

"Don't be coy, Les. This is serious." He turned up Lawrence, a one-way street, and I made frantic noises. "What's the matter?" he asked.

"This is a one-way street."

"Well, I'm only going one way."

"Corn! The arrows are all pointing the other way. You'd better try a different routine on this motorcycle cop."

Napoleon B. pulled over beside a fire hydrant, narrowly missing taking a fender off a parked car. He faced the irate officer, all innocence.

"Something wrong, officer?"

The cop smiled bitterly. "Oh, no," he said with suspect sweetness, "nothing at all, not one little thing. Just a teensy-weensy matter of going the wrong way on a one-way street, parking on the wrong side of the street, and parking next to the fire hydrant." He hadn't a leg to stand on for the latter two counts, but I guess he threw them in for the laughs. Out came the notebook. "And now, if you please, would your lordship be so kind as to allow me to see your driver's license?"

Napoleon B. detests heavy-handed sarcasm.

"Driver's license?" he asked, little eyes as wide as possible. "Do you need a license to drive?"

I thought the cop was going to blow a fuse.

"Move over!" he bellowed. "We're taking a trip to the station."

"O'Halloran," the large man said severely, "the first thing a policeman must learn is to cultivate a sense of humor, a *real* sense of humor." He moved over from the shadows so that the light was on his face for the first time, and added crisply, "I'm on official business, O'Halloran."

The cop fell back, red-faced, and touched his cap. "I'm sorry, Mr. Smith."

Napoleon B. waved a magnanimous hand. "That's all right," he said. "You were only doing your duty."

As we drove off, I said to the fat man, "Look here, you were in the wrong and you know it. You're just helping to break the law. You aren't on official business."

"That," he told me, drawing up before a large greystone house, "remains to be seen."

I took a quick look.

"If you gave me three guesses, Napoleon B., I'd still say this was the Cartwright residence—from what I saw of the pictures in the morgue."

"And each time you'd be right." He wriggled his lard from underneath the wheel. "I hope the young lady doesn't consider it too late to call on her. After all, I am her legal representative."

The old hypocrite!

CHAPTER NINE

Lights were on all over the place. A half-dressed butler, after some hesitation, let us in and conducted us to the drawing room. "Conducted" is a good word, because I often wonder how humans live in these mausoleums of the rich. I would rather be cozy any time.

"I'll tell Miss Cartwright you gentlemen are here," said the butler, hiding a not-quite-tucked-in shirttail.

As he sailed out of the room under bare poles, I grinned at Napoleon B., although I did not feel like grinning. There was an emptiness in me when I thought of that handkerchief.

"Chippendale and Old Colonial," said Napoleon B., paying no attention to me.

"Look at those Ming vases," I groaned. "I couldn't buy them with the price of a dozen books."

"And that Van Gogh original." The detective examined it critically. "The Arlesienne period, I'd say. Say, this is better than the National Art Gallery! Look . . . Corot . . . Rembrandt . . . Reynolds . . . yes, there's a Gauguin!"

It had been some time since I had seen Napoleon B. so excited. He was like a child given free run of a candy shop.

"It must be paradise to live with these things around, Les. I would gaze at them all day if I lived here."

"I'm afraid they'd soon become part of the furniture to you, Mr. Smith." Gale Cartwright spoke from the entrance way. She was dressed in some pale-blue thing that matched her eyes and, at the moment, most of her complexion. But she appeared quite composed. "You'll have to pardon me. I've just had the most dreadful news."

The large man nodded briskly. "About your brother, you mean?"

She was startled. "How . . . how did you know?"

He continued to eat up a striking Grant Wood and said, without turning around, "Oh, we were there." I tried not to notice as the poor girl staggered visibly. "Whoever chose these pictures had a catholic taste."

"I . . . I chose most of them. What do you . . ."

"Then I admire your taste as much as my friend here admires your person. Mind if I sit down?"

She gave him assent with a weak movement of one hand. Napoleon B., as was his habit, picked out the most fragile-looking chair in the room, a creation of gilt and spidery legs and a figured tapestry upholstering. I used to wonder why he did it, but I had long since learned the psychology of it. Persons he was interviewing became so worried over the fate of their precious chairs that they gave him mechanical answers to important questions, and mechanical answers often point the way to truth. To see his huge hulk teetering on that Louis period piece was to think of a cathedral turned upside down and swaying from side to side on its spire. It worked with Gale as with everyone else; she could not take her eyes from the chair.

"Forgive my interruption." The large man dripped honey. "You were saying, Miss Cartwright?"

Without another word she sank down into a convenient settee and began to sob. I was angry with Napoleon B. and showed it.

"Now look what you've done!"

"A woman's refuge and the average man's bafflement." He crossed his huge legs affably and the chair gave an ominous creak, but they knew how to make furniture in the 17th Century. "I am not an average man. Come, Miss Cartwright, dry your pretty eyes. Your brother could not have meant so much to you."

Unexpectedly she shot out, "I thought him a hateful person."

"Then why waste tears on him?"

"Look, Napoleon B.," I attempted to cut in, "can't you question her some other time?"

Gale gave me a grateful look, which isn't the kind I got from the detective. "Thank you, Mr. Allen," she sobbed. "I . . . I knew you . . . you'd understand."

"I'm afraid, Miss Cartwright, that Mr. Allen is way off base. He's a soft touch, but *I'm hard*. Yet I'm not too hard. I know a lady, I mean a real woman, when I see one, and you have my complete sympathy, no matter what you've done." Napoleon B. Smith began the painful process of heaving himself from his seat. "No matter what."

That got her.

"Please, Mr. Smith, I don't understand."

"This afternoon, my dear, you appointed me as your legal representative. Tonight, things have happened. I asked you a question to which my interfering friend here," with venom, "objected. I would like an answer to that question. I repeat it: why waste tears on your detested brother?"

She had out a handkerchief again. It was a twin to the one now in the detective's possession.

"Because . . . because of the way he went . . . the police . . . you . . . so soon after Mother . . . so soon after what happened to her."

Napoleon B. smiled benignly, as a teacher would on a responsive pupil. "Ah, now we begin to understand one another, Miss Cartwright. Indeed we do!" He held up a warning hand, as she seemed about to speak further. "Before you say anything more, let me warn you of something. I have no right to ask you questions. You need not answer them. This is a case for the Homicide Bureau. As yet, my dear, nobody but Mr. Allen and I are aware of your connection with the matter. And we, I can promise you, are the souls of discretion . . . up to a point."

The lovely girl stiffened. The handkerchief was twisted between her two hands. "My connection with the matter?" she asked frigidly. "Just what do you mean, Mr. Smith?"

I always hated Napoleon B. when he was cruel. At the moment he was detestable to me. He was an overfed tomcat with a pretty, little, frightened mouse.

"Need we be playful, Miss Cartwright? However, if you are willing to do me a favor, I shall be pleased to forget all about it . . . unless I am called upon by the gendarmerie to refresh my memory, an unlikely event."

He could talk like a college professor with some, and like a stevedore with others. Once a cynic dubbed him, "Chameleon." He rather liked that; it suited his vanity. He always said that what made him a good detective was that he had no conscience. I wouldn't have gone that far; I would have said he had a conscience only when it suited him.

But she gave him back almost as good as he dished out, lifting her eyebrows viciously and asking sweetly, "Blackmail, Mr. Smith?"

He shrugged his great shoulders, obviously unmoved, while the palms of my hands sweated. When the silence got too deep for her, she lifted her head above it and went on, "What is this favor, Mr. Smith?"

"It's a small thing but it means a lot to me. It means my vindication to myself. I have been refused the request once already today. I trust you will not try my patience to the extent of refusing me also." He paused, then said, "Miss Cartwright, I want you to request the district attorney for permission to exhume your mother's body."

It was as though he had struck her, and I did not like to look at her hurt—it showed in every sag of her face and body.

"You don't know what you're asking," she began faintly.

"I am asking complete peace of mind, which is more important to me at the moment than your welfare."

"But . . . but Mother always had a horror of autopsies. She told me many, many times that when she was b . . . buried she wanted to remain . . . that way."

The little eyes of the big man were hard. "That's what *you* say." He came and stood over her, and anyone watching would have known she was afraid. "There's nobody to verify that now, not even your brother. Would it not be better to have your mother exhumed than, for example, to be arrested yourself for murder?"

The detective spat out the last word. This time she crumpled completely.

"You don't know what you're saying . . . you don't know what you're saying," she repeated.

"Perhaps not, but . . ." He held the wisp of handkerchief in his hand. It looked very tiny there, yet somehow I could only think of it as a rope around her pretty neck. ". . . you might have a hard time explaining to the district attorney how this handkerchief of yours came to be lying beside the body of the brother you hated."

"I'm sorry, Les," he apologized, breaking the uneasy silence between us, as we drove off downtown. "I *had* to do it. I'm not turning her in yet, anyway. Les, do you hear me?"

I heard him all right, but I wasn't talking.

CHAPTER TEN

The next day Napoleon B. Smith went about his own affairs and I went about mine. I found it very hard to forgive him for his latest escapade. If I could have seen the sense in it—but to frighten the poor girl when she was obviously in a jam as it was, for some obscure purpose of his own, struck me as a new low even for the large man. I had no personal interest in the affair, of course, but was thinking solely of Miss Cartwright's welfare.

All day, that handkerchief kept sticking itself under my mental nose and blowing. It was her handkerchief, there was no doubt about it. I thought back to the scene the night before, when she had said tearfully, "But Mr. Smith, Mr. Allen, you *must* believe me! I lost that handkerchief today after leaving the lawyer's office. I must have dropped it somewhere, someone picked it up, and . . ."

"And took it and conveniently dropped it at the scene of your brother's murder," Napoleon B. had finished for her. "I'm certain the police will believe you. Of course, while I make no guarantees, if I had the exhumation order I might forget to tell the police about this for a while."

"How very noble of you, Mr. Smith," she had flamed, "trading upon the miseries of a woman. I am certain you must feel very proud of yourself. Mr. Allen, I have a feeling you don't approve of this."

I had had the same feeling myself, but I had not cared to express it with Napoleon B. so clearly on the trail and nosing.

"I see." She had sneered at me enough to scorch. "I know at last a synonym for jellyfish, Mr. Allen. Well, Mr. Smith, I am only one woman, alone and in need of friends. I suppose I must make the best of a bad job. Before I consent to what you ask, I would like to ask you one thing: do you believe me guilty of murder?"

"Murder is a harsh word, my dear," Napoleon B. had said with unwonted gentleness. "At the moment, I would call it justifiable homicide."

She had suddenly become very pathetic, even to him, but with a dignity of hopelessness we both felt.

"Mr. Smith, you have been accused lately of something you swear you did not do, but which everybody believes you did do." She had had the large man there, and his interest in her had quickened. "I will make you a sporting proposition. If I consent to the exhumation of my mother's body, will you take my case for me?"

"I am still your representative, Miss Cartwright," he had reminded her, and then spoiled it all by adding, "but, of course, my time is valuable and . . ."

"Ten thousand dollars for my proof of innocence of murder, Mr. Smith!" she had said sharply.

Napoleon B's smile had been fangy. "You value your life cheaply, my dear, for one who will inherit millions from your brother's untimely death." I had not thought of that before. "No doubt he died intestate, if I know the type. It might be, of course, that Mr. Handley will fight the will, but . . ."

The red had come into her cheeks in two scarlet spots. "You may leave him out of this, Mr. Smith. No matter how much I detest you and your . . . uh . . . friend here at the moment, I am also conscious of your great ability. Your ability would have to be great to make up for your cruel rudeness." The detective had bowed gravely in acknowledgment of the tribute. "I shall make the offer twenty-five thousand dollars, and consider it cheap at twice that price. But the offer is contingent upon results."

"Naturally. May I have it in writing?"

That last was what had hurt most, the knowledge that he did not trust this lovely, helpless girl. That was why I was not speaking.

Napoleon B. came in late in the afternoon with a fat smile on his fat face and rubbing his fat hands together. The sight disgusted me so much I almost split an infinitive.

"How's the *Case of the Twin Daggers* coming along?" he demanded gleefully.

"I have dropped that for the time being," I told him with dignity. "I am now at work on my great novel."

"Someday you're going to finish more than a chapter of that, Les," he said, amicably enough.

"Well, I find it very hard to write about you when I can't stand you!"

He laughed. He always laughs the hardest when I am at my most serious.

"A good, healthy hate never hurt anyone, least of all a writer," he said. "In fact, I should think hate would be more conducive to good writing than love." He looked at me keenly. "Or does this happen to be a mixture of both?" He saw that it was, and groaned, "Not again! Look here, Les, I hate to come between you and your sudden romances, but that girl is out of your class anyway, so why treat me like a heel?"

"Because you are one," I answered evenly.

"I'm only trying to make an honest living. That girl needs me, you'll grant that." I nodded against my will. *I'm* taking all the risks. No clearance of murder suspicions, no money. If I clear her, twenty-five grand will be chicken feed to her."

I did not like the way he said that "if."

"You believe her guilty yourself!" I accused.

"I never believe any of my clients guilty until hung. You know that. But I have to be realistic about this. And we're on a spot, too, Les. You were the one who took the handkerchief, remember? If we're ever forced to turn it in, I'm afraid even you couldn't explain your way out of it, not even with a plea of amnesia."

He had me there. I hadn't thought of that. Or at least I had thrust it into the back of my mind, not wanting to think about it.

"But right here in my pocket, my lad," he continued, giving his breast a resounding wallop, "I have the solution to all our problems, or at least I'd give odds on it. Miss Cartwright just signed the exhumation order before Dr. Bryce and the district attorney. Coming?"

"Ghoul!" I bit at him, but he knew I could no more resist following him on a case than I could help following a blonde on the street.

The summer sun was dipping into the low hills as we chugged into the ornamental gateway at Woodlawn Memorial Park. Somehow, the dusk breeze seemed a trifle chillier after we had passed through the gates into the cool green beyond, broken by the ghosts of headstones and the pale colors of dying flowers. I shivered a bit. Cemeteries have no attraction for me whatsoever; my will leaves instructions for me to be cremated. Napoleon B. has a theory that cemeteries, as such, will disappear by the year 2000 A.D. The land will be needed for the living, he says. He calls cemeteries a sad economic waste, and points to all the office buildings that lie heavy on the chests of worn-out churchyard cemeteries in the large cities.

"The Cartwright Mausoleum?"

The attendant touched his cap respectfully as we mentioned so much wealth. "Turn right here to the first roadway, then turn left there, and go on straight, down. You can't miss it, sir. It's at the end of a small lane of poplars. There's an angel with folded wings atop it. Is there anything wrong, sir? The police car just went in."

"It's quite all right," the large man reassured him, tipping him magnificently with a dime. I blushed as we drove on.

The gloom deepened, the farther we penetrated the place. Napoleon B. whistled Dixie tunelessly, which showed he was worried about something. Now the shadows were long from the poplars. Suddenly we came to a dark grove, practically roofed over with elm. An ugly granite and marble structure squatted in the leafy enclosure, held down by a weighty angel with folded bronze wings and a smug expression of sanctity that even the gathering night could not hide. This, I said to myself, could happen only to a millionaire. It is an affront to architecture and to God.

"That's funny," said Napoleon B.

"What?"

His hand swept the empty grove. We were alone. As we were puzzling over this and wondering what had happened to the police car mentioned by the attendant, an automobile

drove up behind us. Inspector Joe Brownlee heaved himself
out of the front seat.

"Beat us to it, eh?" he asked, quite genially for him.

"But I thought . . ." The large man stopped. "Where's
the other police car?"

"*What* other police car?"

Without another word, Napoleon B. turned and lum-
bered for the mausoleum. The Inspector, used to such reac-
tions on the part of the detective, unholstered his gun and
followed. I had taken one or two steps in the same direction
when a long, black car drove up and joined the semicircle.
It was the Cartwright limousine. Gale Cartwright's white
face showed in the dim interior. She beckoned me over re-
servedly.

"I just happened to think, Mr. Allen," she said, "that you
couldn't get into the tomb without this key. There are only
two, and my step . . . my brother has . . . had the other." She
paused. "I insist upon witnessing the exhumation."

I called out to Napoleon B. to hold everything, and as-
sisted the lovely girl from the automobile before her chauffeur could rouse himself. She looked frail and helpless in
black, but there was steel in the arm I held. She flashed me
a grateful smile.

"I'm afraid I was quite rude last night," she said.

The shoe, I assured her, was on the other foot. But I
protested her intention of watching them open her mother's
coffin. It was not, I told her, a pretty sight, even for hardened police officers. She could wait outside.

Flashlights were now bobbing all over the place.

"For gosh sake, watch everything!" Napoleon B. called
out angrily. "You'll destroy footprints and tire tracks if
you're not careful."

"What does he mean?" Gale asked me.

That *Nuit de Joie* perfume of hers certainly did things to me. She now had my arm tucked up against her softness as we walked along, and I put my feet down upon air with care. It was silly, I told myself, an only moderately well-to-do hack walking arm in arm with millions and thrilling to the voice of a girl who might have murdered her own brother—especially walking in a graveyard to open her mother's coffin. But then I never have cared where or how I fell in love, the end results being the only things that interested me.

"Another police car was supposed to have come up here ahead of us," I said. "The only thing is, the police don't know anything about it."

"What are we getting into, Mr. Allen?" She sounded frightened and bewildered, and she clung to me very softly, or was I imagining things again? "Why are all these dreadful things happening? Surely . . . surely nobody would touch mother's coffin."

Yet I knew she had the answer to that as much as I; such things can and do happen when the reason is great enough. And her car, with the silent chauffeur, where had it come from so suddenly? Was the key she had handed me her reason for being there? I felt in my heart of hearts that there were other keys, figurative ones, that Gale Cartwright could supply to the rapidly growing Cartwright riddle.

"Hurry up! Hurry up! We haven't all night, Les!" Napoleon B. barked at me. I hadn't realized how slowly, how reluctantly, we were strolling toward the massive door of the last Cartwright mansion, built for eternity.

I held up the key Gale had given me and Napoleon B. practically snatched it from my hands. I noticed he had put on rubber gloves, and Brownlee had an ordinary leather pair. The latter held the flashlight while Napoleon B. inserted the heavy, intricate key. After a few seconds of

wiggling, the great lock clicked. The door swung protesting-
ly open to the large man's push. It must have been two feet
thick. Napoleon B. took two or three cautious steps inside.

"Hmmmmm!" he commented, and again "Hmmmmm!"

"Something wrong, Napoleon B.?" called Brownlee.

"Ask Miss Cartwright if this vault is air-conditioned."

Miss Cartwright called back that it wasn't, that her
father hadn't believed in such things.

"Then somebody's been here recently. The air is fresh.
Come on in." As an afterthought, for which we are all for-
ever grateful, he added, "Post a man outside, Joe, to watch
the cars. There's something funny going on. What brought
you here, Miss Cartwright?"

The last was said very gruffly. He was in a tearing temper
about something. I know how he hates to be outguessed and
outmanoeuvred.

"The key," she answered composedly, "with which you
have just unlocked the door."

"Ah, yes, the key. Thank you. It was most . . . uh . . .
convenient of you. Now that you're here, would you mind
telling us which is your mother's coffin?"

Her finger trembled as it pointed out a very handsome
mahogany casket.

"There's an electric light in here somewhere," she said.
Napoleon B.'s flash picked out the switch and Brownlee
clicked it. The place was flooded with a soft light, taking
away some of the macabre atmosphere. Gale showed up
under it very pale and somehow not as pretty as formerly. It
may have been the strain.

Brownlee was saying, "If I only knew some of what it
was all about, Napoleon B.; I don't know why you keep us
in the dark."

"Didn't I just let some light into the darkness?" The fat man smiled complacently. "Joe, it's the truth; I know as little as you do about it."

The Inspector groaned. "No fingerprints, no clues, no nothing. And now this silly business of the old dame." He recollected himself. "Excuse me, miss. I forgot."

Napoleon B. was examining the casket with interest. He told one of the policemen to get a screwdriver.

While we waited, Brownlee went on complaining. "The Police Commissioner will be on my tail if I don't get some action on this case," he said. "Napoleon B., are you sure you're not holding out on me?"

"Have I ever, Joe?" countered the detective.

"Every time I've had anything to do with you. But you've always kicked through in the end."

"Then let's leave it that way."

Gale Cartwright was leaning against me weakly, for support, I supposed; for other reasons, I hoped. Brownlee turned his attention to her.

"Can't you, Miss Cartwright, as the papers say, shed any light on the mysterious slaying of your brother? I'm Inspector Joseph Brownlee of the Homicide Bureau, by the way."

"I'm afraid not, Inspector," she answered quite composedly, but the slight tremor of her nervousness communicated itself to me with an unpleasant shock. "We did not get along very well together. I scarcely saw him."

"Aren't you surprised at your stepmother leaving him all that money when he was so wild?"

"She was very indulgent with him. My father worshipped Jack from the time he was a baby, and this feeling was communicated by my father's stronger nature to my stepmother. That is the only explanation I can give."

"But she practically cut you off—you who had looked after her so much—and left the money to two persons not very concerned about her in her lifetime." Brownlee all but leered. "Inconsistent, don't you think, Miss Cartwright?"

"I think," she answered coldly, "that your insinuations are all the more in poor taste, Inspector, when you consider where you are."

Napoleon B., who for once had been silent, clapped his big hands together soundlessly.

"Touché, my dear Brownlee," he said, and the way he said it was an insult. "And besides, Miss Cartwright, as your representative, I advise you to answer no more questions."

"Her *what?*" exploded the Inspector.

"Miss Cartwright has been kind enough to entrust me with her affairs." The fat man was at his suave best. "Ah, there you are, Tom." I think he knew every policeman in the city by his first name. "Just take the screws out of the lid and lift it, if you don't mind."

We were all quiet, as though by common consent. The mausoleum was a huge place, as private tombs go, and we waited at the one end for no particular reason, while the policeman methodically removed the screws.

"They've been oiled not long ago," he said, as he took one out. "Here, catch!"

He threw a screw to Napoleon B. Smith who caught it expertly and examined it with a frown.

"The lid's stuck a bit," said Tom.

They were the last words he ever said. There was a blinding flash of lights and a cacophony that melted into a confusion of nothingness. My last thought was that the building seemed to be collapsing.

CHAPTER ELEVEN

"Booby-trapped!"

Napoleon B. Smith was striding up and down our hospital room waving a bandaged hand furiously. It was five days later, and his first day up. The doctor said I could get up in the afternoon. My plates had shown there were no internal injuries, as had been feared, but I was still suffering considerably from shock. Some of the newspapers were calling me "hero" because I had thrown myself on top of Gale Cartwright, saving her from serious injury, but I did not feel heroic about it; I knew it had been purely an instinctive reaction.

"And I fell for it!" Napoleon B. assailed himself bitterly. "Without even thinking, I fell for it. It could just as easily have been me as Tom. In fact, it was meant for me." He stopped his pacing and threw the uninjured left index finger at me. "Les, the murderer wanted to rub me out; I was the only one who guessed something. But I'm not dead, and just as soon as I'm out of here I'm going to get on the job." He fretted, "I just hope the trail isn't cold."

I could understand how he felt, but I was too weak to work up much of a hate, especially as Gale walked in at that

moment, loaded down with flowers, candy, books, and all
the things that visitors bring to hospitals for patients who
are too ill to enjoy them. I thanked her and she smiled at
me in a way that sent my temperature up to boiling point.
Napoleon B. stopped his pacing to glare at her.

"Here she is," he said sarcastically, "still all very nicely
put together because I have a blasted fool for a partner.
Good morning, Miss Cartwright. What fresh trouble have
you for us this fine day?"

"Ignore him," I told her. "He got up out of the wrong
side of the bed this morning twice. And thanks for everything. It's very sweet of you."

"It's very sweet of you, it's very sweet of you," mimicked
Napoleon B., sitting down heavily on the white hospital bed
so that the spring practically had all the give taken out of it.

"Why, Mr. Smith," the girl laughed, "I do believe you're
jealous!"

The big walrus eyed her with aversion, deliberately
turned his back on us, and went on with his reading of *Das
Kapital*, which he claims he reads through once every year.
I can believe it, too. He's the same kind of reader as was T.
E. Lawrence, if not as prolific.

We went on talking in low tones, Gale apparently vastly
amused by the large man. Presently, there was a snort from
the bed, and a barely audible, "Booby-trapped!"

It was preying on him, this feeling that he had failed,
where an ordinary man would have congratulated himself
upon an extraordinary escape from death. An angle in the
vault had taken the main force of the blast away from us,
but the concussion in that confined space had been terrific.
Tom, the policeman, whose lifting of the lid had set off
the potent charge of T.N.T., had been literally blown apart.
The rest of us were injured in various ways and knocked

unconscious. The force of the explosion had blown shut and wedged the massive mausoleum door. Deadly fumes from the nitroglycerin in that airless atmosphere seemed to have doomed us all. What had saved us had been Napoleon B. Smith's foresight in posting a lookout. The sentry policeman had been alert and well-trained, and had used a Tommy gun to blast the hinges off the door so that it fell outwards of its own weight. Inhalator crews had to go to work on all of us, but poor Tom Jenkins had been the only fatality.

"And a good man gone." The fat man went on seemingly talking to himself. "All because I drove a golf ball into the rough. All because a little old lady . . ."

He slammed the book shut, hoisted himself around to look at us. "There was nobody there," he said, glaring at us for contradiction. "The murderer is smart and has accomplices. Accomplices—one or more, because the cemetery attendant can't remember how many—were in that stolen police car in those stolen police uniforms. Do you know what I'm thinking, Miss Cartwright?"

She shook her head somewhat apprehensively. Unexpectedly he smiled, the smile of a child about to give away a precious piece of candy.

"I don't believe that a murderer would walk into a vault she thought was going to be blown sky-high."

"Thank you, Mr. Smith." Gale's voice was low. "Now perhaps you believe I *did* lose my handkerchief."

"I believe nothing except evidence. Les will tell you that, my dear. But I also have a heart." This was a surprising admission. "Joe Brownlee told me about the check."

"Check?" I pricked up my ears.

"Ten thousand dollars to Tom Jenkins' widow and family." Napoleon B. cleared his throat noisily. "That was very nice of you, Gale."

When he used her first name I knew she was accepted. She gave him a warm glance I wish she had saved for me.

"However, my dear," he continued, "there's something I must say to you. I feel that, for some strange reason, or perhaps the reason may not be so strange in the light of human illogic, you are in very grave danger. I would ask you to be frank with me for a change."

The lovely girl got up at this and went to stand at the window. It was open on to a grand summer's day. She leaned on the window sill, looking out. I gazed at Napoleon B. reproachfully, but his large countenance was serene.

Suddenly he bounded from the bed and flung himself across the room, knocking Gale onto her back beside the window and letting out a howl as he injured his hand anew. In the same split second, something pinged by my head and bit into the plaster near my bed light.

I was already reaching for the telephone when Napoleon B. bellowed, "Get out of bed first, you fool! Roll out!" I did it, with the telephone in my hand. The operator thought I was nuts when I told her to get me the police, but some choice words convinced her. Brownlee said he'd be there before I hung up. It wasn't a minute, I'm sure, until I heard police sirens all over the adjoining streets. Those babies sure can throw a cordon fast.

Gale was out cold. Napoleon B. never could learn how to tackle women. He was cursing methodically over his aching hand and vowing all kinds of spectacular vengeance. I had reached up and switched my bed signal, and the nurse had come rustling in and was staring at us very disapprovingly.

"This is no way to act in a hospital," she said coldly, "and as for you, miss . . ."

But her professional eye soon saw what was amiss and she did not wait for explanations. I demanded one from Napoleon B.

"Pure luck, son. I saw the sunlight glint on something in that window on the opposite court. I guess I'm getting trigger-happy, because I immediately thought 'rifle' and dived for Gale. Sorry I hit her so hard."

"I guess she'll be glad when she hears about it. Do you mind helping me back into bed, nurse?"

That's the first time in my life a woman ever helped me into bed.

The doctor came, and a few walking patients whom the nurse shooed out, and then handsome Cyrus Handley.

"Hi, everybody," he said from the doorway, and then saw something was wrong with Gale. They had laid her on Napoleon B's bed. "What's happened?"

"She came very close to having daylight let into her. Target practice." I could see something in Napoleon B's eye. "Where'd *you* come from, Mr. Handley?"

"Never mind that." The tall fellow was brusque. I could see he was quite agitated. "Is she all right? Did anything happen?"

"Napoleon B. was quicker than a bullet." I said.

"I was just on my way to pay you fellows a visit."

"From across the court?" growled Napoleon B.

Handley seemed puzzled. "I'm afraid I don't understand, Mr. Smith."

"Skip it. We can check on you later. How about looking at my hand, doctor?"

While the doctor clucked over the detective's ham of a hand that was beefsteak raw with the bandage off, Gale opened her eyes. The first person she saw was her stepcousin, Cyrus Handley. I knew right away I didn't have a chance. It spilled all over from her eyes; she just couldn't hold it in.

"Cy!" she whispered. "Oh, Cy darling, I'm so glad you came!"

Then she passed out again. I wished I could have done the same. My heart had a fracture job on it no doctor could ever mend.

Joe Brownlee was so mad the flint of his eyes was striking sparks.

"Not a whisper, not a trace!" he moaned. "That gun has to be somewhere in this hospital. Whoever did the shooting was cute enough to use a silencer and pick up the discarded shell. If this keeps up, Napoleon B., I'll lose my job sure."

The fat man waved a freshly bandaged hand in disgust. "You're just lucky you haven't another unsolved murder on your hands, that's all, Joe. Let me have another look at that bullet you dug out of the plaster."

It was a flat, misshapen thing. Napoleon B. hummed over it deprecatingly.

"Do you mind if I have a look, Mr. Smith?" asked Cyrus Handley genially. Gale was sitting propped up in bed, and Cyrus had to disengage her hand in order to take the bit of lead the detective passed to him without comment. "As you gentlemen may or may not know, I'm a bit of an expert on firearms. I've been doing a lot of experimenting with German air rifles." He looked up, his handsome face serious. "It's just as I suspected. This is a pellet from a high-powered air rifle."

"Kid stuff!" snorted Inspector Brownlee. "Now they're wishing air rifles on me. You can't kill with *air* rifles."

Handley objected instantly. "Oh, but you can, Inspector. Indeed you can. Why, the Germans were making air rifles with more penetrating power than .32 calibre revolvers and at greater target distances. Some of our models, I can say with modesty, are even more efficient." He turned to Gale with a worried smile, "I hate to say this, dear, but our firm may even have made the rifle that this bullet came from."

"Any way you can tell, Mr. Handley?" asked Napoleon B.

The young man shook his head. "An air rifle won't conform to the usual ballistics tests. In fact, I know of no way that a bullet from an air rifle could be identified." He flashed a real smile this time. "And air rifles can be camouflaged so readily. For instance, I carry one in this walking stick of mine."

I had noticed the affectation but had not paid it much attention. "You mean there's a rifle in that walking stick?" I asked. "Aren't you taking an awful chance telling us that?"

Maybe it was malicious. Handley went dead white, and he half rose. Napoleon B. waved him back languidly.

"Les means nothing by it, Mr. Handley. He just shoots off his face. Mind if I examine the . . . uh . . . weapon?"

"Not at all." Did Handley actually sound too eager, or was it my jealous imagination? "But be careful; it's loaded. The safety catch is on."

"Can't you unload it?"

"Only by firing. It's a simple mechanism, as you may not know. My models use compressed air for velocity and distance. Yet I defy you to tell this from an ordinary walking stick."

The Inspector and Napoleon B. were intent on the walking-stick weapon, and Handley obviously liked talking about his work. I stole a glance at Gale. She was staring in horrified surprise at Cyrus Handley until she felt me looking; then she veiled her eyes, But I knew what was running through her mind—it was galloping through mine, too.

Cyrus Handley could inherit everything with Gale out of the way. He was a skeet-shooting champion. He manufactured air rifles. He was in the hospital when the shooting occurred. It would have been simple for him, and by far the safest procedure, to duck around the corridors and into our room. We had learned that the room from which the shooting had probably taken place was vacant. It was a private room, paid for in advance by someone unknown but who had never occupied it, and whose name of "John Armstrong" was obviously as phony as the nonexistent address he had given.

"An interesting weapon," said Napoleon B. professionally, "and a nice-looking cane, too. Incidentally, I don't believe that shot was meant for Miss Cartwright at all. I believe *I* was the intended victim, but my sudden movement to rescue Gale saved my own life. Somebody thinks I know too much."

What was he trying to give me? Did he know what I was thinking, and was he trying to warn me to keep my mouth shut? There was no sign from him that could have told.

The nurse bustled in to say that her patients must rest and that, police or no police, everyone would have to leave. If Miss Cartwright wished, there was a spare room in the women's ward on the next floor.

Gale shook her head unhappily. "I'm quite all right, thank you. I . . . I'm going home."

Handley jumped up. "I'll see you home, dear."

To my hypersensitive eyes the idea seemed to frighten her.

"No, thanks, Cy. I'll telephone John and have him meet me with the car."

She reached for the telephone, but waited as a rap came on the door. It was a tall, red-faced young policeman.

"Pardon me, Inspector," he said formally, and I thought how policemen with college educations are no asset to crime, "but I began to think, and . . ."

"You know that's against the regulations, Hunter," the Inspector cut in, not unkindly. "In my day . . . oh well, go on, what is it?"

"This, sir." He held up a bundle wrapped in a sheet. "I began to put myself in the criminal's place, as they say, and . . ."

"Get to the point, Hunter, get to the point," said the Inspector impatiently.

"Well, sir, I reasoned that if I wanted to get rid of something in a hurry in a hospital, I'd wrap it in a sheet and . . ."

"Drop it down the laundry chute," rumbled Napoleon B. "Very commendable, young man. Well, let's see the air rifle."

Deflated, the cop unwrapped the sheet. Nestled in its white folds was a complex looking weapon.

"One of our better models," said Cyrus Handley.

"I'll see this is mentioned in the report, Hunter," the Inspector told the cop, who brightened at that "Don't mind Mr. Smith. He likes pricking balloons. When he said 'very commendable' to you, that's like a medal from the Police Commission. Get it dusted for fingerprints."

"Please, sir," the young man blushed deeply, "I've already taken the liberty of having that done. The gun was wiped clean, probably with the sheet."

"You can retire any time, Joe;" said Napoleon B. ironically. "Youth must be served."

I thought the same thing, but for different reasons. Gale had suddenly begun to live again. She had put the telephone back.

"I've changed my mind, Cy," she said, and her voice was like the notes of a flute. "I'd *love* to have you drive me home."

Napoleon B. raised his eyebrows at me, but I was past sympathy.

CHAPTER TWELVE

A couple more days had gone by and the doctors had let us go home to "rest." This was always a purely conjectural matter with Napoleon B. Smith. As for myself, I was genuinely depressed; Gale Cartwright had not been anywhere near me since the day of the shooting.

"Oh, for crying out loud!" Napoleon B. exploded at me mildly. He was taking golf swings in the middle of the room, holding the club gingerly with his injured hand. "Snap out of it, Les! This is about the umpty-umpth time You've been in love."

"But never this way," I groaned hollowly.

"That's what you say every time. Remember the case of the Hot Tamales, and little Chiquita, the dancer? When she left you for that Gonzales fellow you went into a decline even more rapid than this one. Then there was the time that that little redheaded Clara . . ."

"Oh, shut up, Napoleon B.," I said. "This time it's different."

"Well, if you enjoy your suffering . . ." He shrugged his shoulders. "Here now, tell me what I'm doing wrong with this swing." He swung back tentatively.

"Your feet are all wrong, and that's not a baseball bat—that's a driver. You're bending your elbows. You're not keeping your eye on the ball. Outside of all that, you're one hundred per cent correct." The irony was wasted. The club head was coming down. "At least you can follow through. Go on. Follow through!"

Well, I never had liked that chandelier.

"At least," said the large man ruefully, eyeing the pieces, "you must admit I followed through."

We began to laugh, and suddenly I felt better. Then we howled. We were friends again.

"I really thought you were a goner this time," said Napoleon B. when we caught our breath. "I could just see you eating off gold plates, taking the poodles for their daily walk, and living on an allowance from your doting wife. Then when I saw her and Handley together in the hospital that day, I knew you hadn't a chance. I was afraid, though, you didn't know it."

"I did, though. She's a lovely girl."

Napoleon B. looked grave. "Too lovely! And she knows too much." He put the golf club back in the bag thoughtfully. "Les, that girl knows too much for her own good. And so do I. But the trouble is, I don't know what it is that I know. It's like trying to fit together a jigsaw puzzle without all the pieces."

"Tell me."

He creaked himself into his oversize easy chair, lay back, closed his eyes, put the tips of his fingers together as well as he could with the interfering bandage.

"The whole thing has a pattern, and yet the pattern does not make sense," he began. "We've learned that most murders are simple things. They stem from some fundamental emotion—hate, fear, greed, passion . . . even love. They usually revolve around a certain set of persons, except in cases of unpremeditated murder or killing during an armed robbery. Those persons have motives; they leave clues. They are not nearly as clever as they think they are." He broke off. "Say, do you mind getting me that brick of ice cream from the 'fridge? . . . the Neapolitan, not the butterscotch."

I did as he asked, and got myself a Cuba Libra at the same time. I was feeling much better.

He slupped contentedly over the large dish for a while, then went on, spooning himself a mouthful from time, to time. "What is the pattern in this case so far? The pattern is the Cartwrights. There's something in the Cartwright story we don't know that we must know. We have a number of questions to answer. The big question in my mind at the moment is: what happened to old Mrs. Cartwright's body? We know it wasn't in the coffin. If it had been in the coffin, there would have been bits of it mixed up with poor Tom. But the murderer was too canny for that. He knows the freak effects of explosions. He knows that the blast might have blown up the whole place without touching the body, and that means there's something incriminating about that body. Yet we can't find it, and a body is the hardest thing in the world to hide, especially one that's been dead some time. It's been buried again somewhere, probably in a pauper's field, if I know the way this murderer thinks.

"Now, the murderer didn't think up that business of the booby trap on the spur of the moment. He knew . . . why do I keep saying 'he'? It might just as well be 'she'. In any event, he knew that I was coming to exhume the body. He knew I was on to something. But he needed only a few minutes to remove a body and to place the explosive charge. What safer way is there to perform those operations than as a policeman, arriving in a police car? Joe Brownlee's sore as hell over that police car being stolen. He considers it a disgrace to the Force." Napoleon B. chuckled hugely. "Two fat police officers, too fond of playing checkers when they should be on duty in their prowler, are today walking beats that are long, hard, and out-of-the-way. Perhaps it will teach them a lesson."

"None of it seems to make sense," I objected. "And while you're coming clean, how about coming clean all the way? What about Gale's handkerchief? What about what Marcel Leblanc said to you that night in Jack Cartwright's apartment?"

Napoleon B. licked the last spoonful of ice cream with regret. "Murders never work out logically," he evaded, "because murders are illogical. When Cain killed Abel he did so from jealous rage. It would have been a simple matter for Adam, if he had been a detective, to figure out the murderer in that case. You know from stories of our cases that you've written that some murders go along step by step to an inevitable conclusion, evidence piling on evidence, while others remain baffling until the simple solution strikes like lightning. In this Cartwright case you have the paradox of too few persons involved. Thus far we have only Cyrus Handley and Gale Cartwright, and there's more evidence at present pointing to their innocence than to their guilt. Apart from these two, ourselves and the police, we have Dr. Bryce, lawyer Johnson and Marcel Leblanc. If we accept the premise that the killings involve something in the past, present, or future of the Cartwright family, where are we left?"

"We are left," I answered coldly, "with my question still unanswered. The night of Jack Cartwright's murder, Joe Brownlee didn't know there was a Gale Cartwright. Since that time he's learned there is. It won't be long until his memory clicks into place. He's going to remember, as I do,

Marcel Leblanc using the word 'Gale' twice while he was talking to you. Then the fat will be in the fire."

"Well, you should fry nicely, Les." His little eyes took on an appearance of frankness. "Marcel Leblanc simply told me that he had heard his master speaking on the telephone and that he assumed he must be talking to his sister as he addressed her as 'Gale.' The valet said he thought Jack was making arrangements to meet his sister that night."

"At his apartment?" I persisted.

"Oh, all right then! At his apartment."

"If Brownlee ever gets hold of this, Gale's going to be arrested."

"And you are, too, son," said Napoleon B. Smith with his dreadful complacency. "Don't you think it's about time we did something, instead of sitting here?"

I agreed.

One difficulty about having Napoleon B. with a crocked hand was that he reluctantly let me drive. While I am not the world's best by any means, I am a good, average chariot-eer. But to hear Napoleon B. talk, I am the proverbial loose nut at the wheel. I have noticed that invariably the worst drivers are the most nervous when someone else is driving.

"Now, now," he would adjure me, "take it easy, take it easy! Watch where you're going! There's a stop street a block away. Look out for that parked car. Look out for that street-car. Look out for that old lady."

This kept up in a steady stream. You can see why I pre-ferred to let him drive. The purgatory of his driving was as nothing to the hell of his not driving.

But today, perhaps out of a perverse sympathy for my state of mind, he let me drive almost in peace. As we approached the Cartwright mansion I could not help comparing it with that dreadful mausoleum amongst the poplars and elms of Woodlawn. There was the same air of cold and ugly unreality about it, a denial of life's virtues, and an acceptance of the value of money above all other things. I thought that within lay dead things, too, and that only in Gale Cartwright was there any hope for its survival.

There was another car in the driveway. I skirted it and drew our buggy up before the imposing front entrance. I wondered why they didn't have a lodge keeper, but I had heard how parsimonious old Cartwright was in some things and how lavish in others.

The same butler answered the door as that evening that seemed so long ago. This time he was fully dressed. He appeared nervous and upset. When we asked for Miss Cartwright he opened his mouth to say something, clapped it shut on an unspoken word, opened it to ask us to follow him. We were led to the same drawing room.

At least it was the same drawing room in all but one particular. The last time we had been there Inspector Joe Brownlee had not been occupying an easy chair.

"Come in, come in," he growled. "I've been expecting you. You know your way around here, don't you, Napoleon B.?" The fat man said nothing. "Now don't tell me you were surprised to see me!"

"You're as funny as a broken arm," said Napoleon B. bitterly. "All right, what have you done with her?"

"What did you expect me to do with her?" The Inspector was as smooth as melting butter. "I arrested her, of course—as a material witness, naturally."

"But you can't do that!" I protested.

"You tell the little man, Napoleon B."

"He can," said Napoleon B. steadily. "I guess he wants me to earn my twenty-five grand."

Brownlee stood up menacingly. "I want you to quit stalling and tell me everything you know about this case."

"That's easy." The fat man spoke with evident sincerity. "I know nothing; I guess a lot. Guesses aren't evidence. Have you any evidence?"

I held my breath.

"Just what Marcel Leblanc told you. It's enough to hold her, isn't it?"

I let my breath go out. I wasn't going to the jug yet. Gale had not said anything about the handkerchief!

CHAPTER THIRTEEN

Of course, it was a bluff on Brownlee's part. Gale Cartwright's lawyers had her out in four hours flat on a writ of habeus corpus, and the judge was highly indignant about the whole procedure. Joe went out of that courtroom like a whipped dog.

"I feel sorry for him," said Napoleon B. "I'd have done the same thing in his case. Sometimes you get away with it, sometimes you don't. It's all in the business of being a policeman. But we'll have to have a heart-to-heart talk with that young lady. I hope no bullets interfere this time."

That's how come we drove up to the Cartwright mansion again. It was becoming almost monotonous. However, we were not very cordially received.

"Miss Cartwright is seeing no one, sir," the butler told Napoleon B., opening the door on a chain.

"But she *must* see me!" stormed the large detective. "I have a lot of money wrapped up in her."

"I'm sorry, sir. Those are my orders."

The door slid back into place. Napoleon B. gave one of the white panels a childish kick from sheer resentment. It left a black splotch that shamed me.

"Was that necessary?" I asked, as we got in the car.

"What?" He looked puzzled for a moment, then his fate cleared. "Oh, *that!* Well, maybe not, but that butler looks as though he needs some hard work for a change." He chuckled. "I'd like to see his face when he sees what I've done to his lovely, white door."

I slammed into second, irritated. "Quit acting like a big baby," I said, "and start that alleged brain of yours working. That little Cartwright fool is going to have us in the hoosegow yet."

Napoleon B. held his hands in front of his eyes in mock horror, as I took a corner with two wheels in the air.

"Temper, temper," he chided, as I righted the car with difficulty. "Boy, when you change your tune you really get a new melody, don't you? The girl's just scared, that's all, and you can't blame her. Only she shouldn't be scared of me or you or Brownlee. She should be scared of the murderer because she's probably next on the list . . . or I'm all wet about everything. Drive around the block, then go along Eastern. I'll tell you when to stop."

He said "stop" in front of Herb Woodridge's butcher shop. There isn't much Herb won't do for Napoleon B. since the time the detective proved it wasn't the girl who is now Herb's wife who stole the Meldrum pearls. She had been Mrs. Meldrum's personal maid, you remember, and . . . but that's another story.

Herb led us into the back room and offered us a slug. Napoleon B. refused, but I had a small one that made me gag.

It didn't take the detective long to come to the point. "Is your delivery truck in, Herb?"

"Yeah!" Herb jerked a thumb towards the rear. "Out there; why?"

"I want to borrow it for a couple of hours." I put down my empty glass and stared at him. The poor guy, I told myself. "I also want a couple of your butcher's aprons—not fresh, clean ones from the laundry—but some nicely blood-stained. Then a couple of caps and a side of beef."

Herb took off his cap and scratched his head. "Well, now, Napoleon B.," he said slowly, "I dunno about the side of beef. Ain't got a whole side in the place. But I got a hog I was just gonna cut up."

"That'll do." The detective pulled out a roll of bills regretfully. "I'll pay you for the meat. Wholesale, of course."

After a slight rejection of payment on Herb's part they came to an understanding. Napoleon B. handed me one of the aprons and a cap.

"Put it on," he commanded. He saw the look of distaste on my face. "Go on, it won't kill you. The cap, too. Damned if he doesn't look a butcher to the life, eh, Herby? Okay, Butcher Les, grab the hind end of that pig and follow me. Show us your truck, Herb."

Herb opined he hoped we knew what we was doin', and I echoed him. I noticed Napoleon B. did not favor his injured hand as much when toting the carcass, and wondered how much he had been faking. He is a great sympathy cadger. I was confirmed in this when he took the wheel.

After a series of Napoleonic escapes from disaster, we arrived once again at the Cartwright residence. But this time we followed a neat little sign that arrow-pointed along a side driveway, "Tradesmen's Entrance." Taking some unpremeditated short cuts across the velvet lawn, we finally arrived at the kitchen door. A fat French cook came out to meet us and was about to give us a symphonic arrangement of his impressions of our ancestry when Napoleon B. addressed him in French. Instantly the frowns turned to friendliness, the threatening gestures to beckonings of amiability. He ended up by pointing out to us the way to the cold storage room, and he and Napoleon B. parted with regretful bows while I staggered under the weight of the pig and reflected that I was still not fully recovered from the effects of the explosion. I wondered if, perhaps, this were not true of the detective—if it could not be that the shock had shoved his brain over that borderline between genius and insanity.

However, I was soon disabused of this notion. The chef had scarcely departed when Napoleon B. said, "Here, quick! Throw this stinking thing in here." He opened the door of the cold storage and I rubberlegged in with my burden. "Now get rid of your cap and apron in here, too, and let's hotfoot it upstairs."

"Napoleon B.," I admired, "I take off my cap to you." And I suited the words to action.

Presently we were "proceeding with caution" up what seemed an endless series of staircases.

"How do you expect to find her in this rabbit warren?" I whispered.

"I don't know. Depending on luck, I guess. But if she's in seclusion she'll be on one of the upper floors." He motioned me to silence as a pert personal maid passed by, intent on her own business. "If we go where that girl came from, we should find Gale."

We were about to leave the well of the stairs where we were hiding when a furtive shadow crept along the wall of the landing above. For a brief second the face of the shadow was visible. I felt Napoleon B. beside me go rigid.

"That's Louis Perlotti!" he said in my ear. "Come on!"

I needed no urging. Napoleon B. Smith had the best mental rogues' gallery in the country and Louis Perlotti was a star in that gruesome collection, a thug who hired out for murder and seemed to have a talent for evading capture despite the fact that his picture was hanging in every post office. This may have been because he was a completely nondescript little man who looked like one of any thousand persons you could name offhand. We had run into him once before, and he was bad medicine.

The fat man was bounding up the stairs like a cat, his rubber-soled shoes falling soundlessly on the thick carpet. He slipped his gun into his left hand as he ran, and on his face there was an expression that matched anything Louis Perlotti could dig up for ferocity and cold-blooded desire to kill. I was glad he was a sharpshooter with either hand, and one of the fastest men on the draw the F.B.I. had ever turned out. My own gun was in my hand as I went up about two steps behind him, but I'm never very proud of my performance with any kind of weapon except my typewriter.

A door was open. I heard Gale ask, "Is that you, Carla?" and then Napoleon, B. yell, "Run, Gale, run."

Perlotti whirled to meet us, his lips twisted in a snarl. Without pausing, crouched so that if hit he would fall forward and still be able to keep firing, Napoleon B. cut loose with his artillery. I felt the whisper of Death around us as Perlotti fired simultaneously. I was looking incredulously at a hole torn in the sleeve of Napoleon B's coat. Then something rolled past me on the stairs. It was what was left of the gunman, carried forward by his own momentum of hate even as he died.

The large man did not even look back. He knew he would be lying there instead of Perlotti if his aim had not been good. Before I could get into the room with him he was over to the corner where Gale was crouching. He was absolutely beside himself with rage. Pulling the girl, out by the arm with brute strength, he suddenly released her and began to whipsaw her lovely face with the back of the hand that had so lately held a killer's gun. She screamed.

"Cut it out!" I yelled. "Napoleon B., are you crazy?"

He was paying no attention. The methodical blows were not easy ones.

"The police are in the house." Blow. "They'll be here in a moment." Blow. "I've had enough of your monkey business." Blow. "Are you going to talk?" Blow. "Are you?" Blow. "Are you?"

There was blood on her cheek. It all took only several seconds. He was talking between his teeth. I knew it was no use to interfere.

"Yes!" The word was faint. "Yes!"

The large man flung her back to the floor from the kneeling position to which he had jerked her. He had torn her dress and she covered herself awkwardly.

"Playing?" asked Joe Brownlee pleasantly from the doorway. "Like to pick on somebody your own size, Napoleon B.?"

The detective was coming out of it. He passed a hand in front of his eyes. Then he turned away.

"You want to prefer assault charges against him, Miss Cartwright?" asked the Inspector.

She shook her head. "He . . . he had every right to do it. He saved my life." Her lips were puffing up. "That awful man . . ."

"She means Louis Perlotti," I put in, "not Napoleon B."

"Thanks," said the Inspector dryly. "Well, Mr. Smith, that was a nice bit of gunplay. What are you, psychic?" His voice became very cold. "Or could it be that you've been holding out on me?"

"Keep your shirt on, Joe," he said wearily. "I think Baby here is going to talk at last. Isn't that right, Baby?"

Baby just whimpered.

CHAPTER FOURTEEN

The detective went into the bathroom of Gale Cartwright's suite and came out with a bottle of eau de cologne and some cotton batting. He proceeded to dab liberal quantities over the girl's face. She moaned but said nothing.

"Smelling salts?" he asked briefly.

She made a nod toward a vanity dresser and I rummaged in the drawers until I found the small, crusted vial. I held it under her nose until she gasped. By this time I was weak inside all over again about her, and I could have cheerfully slit Napoleon B's throat. I yearned over her poor, bruised features and the dull black streaks on her cheeks where a touch of mascara had run. Crime, I knew, had no boundaries, and the end justifies any means in the category of a policeman like Napoleon B. Smith, but I could not condone a savage attack on a defenseless woman.

Except she had said she would "talk." She had some kind of confession to make. I knew Napoleon B.; he only grew brutal when the trail was growing cold, when he had little to go on, when he needed action fast.

We helped her to her feet and onto a chair. All this time Joe Brownlee had said nothing. Now he faced the large man grimly.

"This had better be good," he said, "or I'm personally going to give you a going-over for that kid . . . and for trying to make a monkey out of me."

"Your ancestors beat me to it," Napoleon B. flipped, but his mouth was not funny; it was a thin, set line. "Ready to answer questions, Miss Cartwright?"

She managed to move her head up and down. Napoleon B. stood over her. All he needed was the bright light in the eyes and the "goldfish" in his hand to complete the picture.

"Miss Cartwright . . . Gale . . ." he began evenly, "you can think what you like of me. I don't care. If you value a beating above your life, then you should hate me. But surely you must realize you are in the greatest of danger at all times. This latest episode must have convinced you. Miss Cartwright," he added abruptly, "whom are you shielding?"

Her bruised lips moved mechanically. "The dead," she said.

Then she fainted.

Both the Inspector and I demanded that he call it off, but the fat man waved our objections aside with impatience. He carried her to the bed, put pillows under her legs and used eau de cologne freely on the temples while motioning me to get busy with the smelling salts. It was grim. Finally she came around. When she did, she was somewhat hysterical.

"Gale." Napoleon B's voice was as soft and gentle as a doting grandmother. "Listen to me, my dear. You cannot help the dead. The dead are past hurting. But you . . . others . . . there's a murderer on the loose. He's killed twice that we know, and once that we suspect. He's killed twice because a golf ball of mine went into the rough. Otherwise, it might never have gone beyond the original killing, for the original killing was planned as an accidental death. Gale, who is the murderer?"

"I don't know; really I don't," she said with difficulty. There was a hint of a smile. "Maybe *I* am."

"You're my client, in spite of everything," Napoleon B. miraculously answered her smile, "and my clients are never guilty. They may be stubborn, beautiful, mistaken, and in need of a thrashing, but they are never guilty."

Joe Brownlee started to say something but the large man glared him quiet. I was hypnotized myself. I never quite become used to Napoleon B's chameleon-like changes.

"I asked you," went on the detective composedly, "whom you were shielding, and you answered 'the dead.' What do you mean?"

"My mother."

Even Napoleon B. was astonished. "But your mother was dead and buried when your brother was shot!" he objected.

"It goes back farther than that, Mr. Smith." She smiled again. "Do you think I could have the pillows under my head now? It's rather . . . uh . . . undignified this way."

I had thought it rather appealing. With a muttered apology, Napoleon B. put the pillows where they belonged, and the girl regained much of the poise she had lost. I noticed Napoleon B. dabbing surreptitiously at his knuckles with the dampened cotton batting. His anger had been no pose, then, assumed for the purpose of extracting information. I thought that if Gale really knew something and had hidden it from us she had given us and herself a great deal of unnecessary trouble and had paid for it dearly.

"What I want to say, Napoleon B.," said Joe Brownlee plaintively, "is that I'm sitting here letting subordinates handle this Louis Perlotti affair. What am I going to tell the newspapers? What am I going to tell the Chief?"

Napoleon B. withered him with, "Tell 'em you didn't have to sit here."

"And have you break the case while I'm looking after dead bodies that you've killed?" the Inspector Irished.

"I'll make a bargain with you," said Napoleon B. "You tell 'em I killed Perlotti—that'll be front page stuff. Then I'll let you break this case. When I have the dope I'll hand it over to you. Fair enough?"

The Inspector nodded and went out.

"That doesn't let you out of that twenty-five grand," the large man told the girl hastily. "I have to eat, you know."

"Obviously!" It's wonderful how quickly a woman can recover her spirits. "I see the Inspector trusts you."

"And you?"

Her fine eyes rested on him for a moment. "I should hate you," she said, "but I don't. You have hardness, but so has a diamond."

I felt very left out of things.

"You said it went farther back, Miss Cartwright," Napoleon B. pursued, "than your mother's death. You said you were shielding your mother. What do you mean?"

Gale was quite composed again, but in a different way. It was quite clear that she had decided to put everything she knew before the fat man. "Do you consider it unnatural, Mr. Smith, for a daughter to hate her father?"

"That all depends," he answered gently, "upon the daughter . . . and upon the father. I've known some fathers it would be very easy to hate."

Gale propped herself upon an elbow and I hastened to make the pillows more comfortable. The detective smiled absently at my eagerness to please.

"I hated my father, Mr. Smith, not momentarily and blindly, as I hated you just now for hitting me, but with a cold-blooded, unrelenting, uninhibited hate. My father was an unfeeling and unthinking brute!"

She spoke with a concentrated venom that showed me a new and rather disquieting side to her character. This was her own flesh and blood about whom she spoke. Napoleon B. was busy making cat tracks on the back of an envelope. He called these "notes," but I never saw him refer to them at any time, though he made them copiously on every case. I think he did it to impress people; his memory was sufficient unto itself.

"I understand Joshua Cartwright was a bit hard to go along with," he said casually.

"A bit hard to get along with!" It was almost an hysterical cry. "Why, the lengths to which that man would go to inflict mental pain on a fellow human being, especially those who should have been dearest to him, were unbelievable!"

"In what way?"

"He *used* people to 'get along,' as he called it. He was a brain-picker. When someone was of no further use to him, he discarded them; sucked them dry and threw them away. My mother—my real mother, not my stepmother—was a lovely, high-spirited woman who loved him devotedly. She brought him a little money which, I am sure, is why he married her in the first place. When the money was in his control he began to treat her unkindly. Oh, he was never so obvious as to beat her; he simply treated her as though she did not exist. To a woman like my mother, that was worse than beating. And he made it known in a thousand different ways that he had no use for me, that he barely tolerated me because it was the expected thing. He was extremely sensitive to outward appearances and thought more of the good opinion of a stranger than of one of his own family." She bit her puffed lip. "In the end, he killed my mother. Nothing that would hold in a court of law, you understand. Legally, she died giving birth to Jack. Morally, he killed her because his indifference and passive cruelty took away from her all desire to live. He *willed* her to die, and she did."

I was engrossed in her story. She was telling it simply, and thus heightening the dramatic effect. Napoleon B. teetered wildly on the boudoir chair, a sure sign of his interest, yes, and his excitement. Pieces of the jigsaw, I could see from his actions, were beginning to turn up and fit.

"In a previous conversation, Miss Cartwright," Napoleon B. prompted her, "you told me that your stepmother was indulgent with your brother because your father had worshipped Jack from the time he was a baby. How does that gibe with what you tell us of your father's character?"

The lovely girl smiled thinly. "You have an excellent memory, Mr. Smith. I recall the statement with difficulty, but I shall accept your word that I made it. I would say it was entirely consistent for my father to lavish what passed in him for affection upon Jack. He saw in the boy an extension of his power, of an ability to cheat death by making Jack in his own image. But he had weak clay. Jack inherited all of my father's weaknesses without any of his crude strengths, all my dear mother's lack of willpower with none of her delicacy of feeling. I think much of Jack's dislike for our stepmother was simply an unconscious aping of Father's desires."

"How did you react to this favoritism by your father?"

"At first it bothered me a great deal, but after a while, when my aversion to my own father became pronounced, it was a matter of supreme indifference to me."

"I see." The detective pursed thick lips. "Believe me, I'm not trying to pry unnecessarily into your rather complicated family affairs. Nor am I subjecting you to a psychiatric examination. That is not in my province, although it might pay you to submit to one at the hands of an expert." The girl flushed deeply at the unconscious insult, but said nothing. "What I am concerned with is motives for murder and, at the moment, I believe the murders are rooted in your family history. I may be wrong, but I must pursue that path to its end. Do you agree?"

Gale Cartwright inclined her head without speaking.

"Did your father become wealthy through the use of your own mother's money?"

"Moderately so. He had a certain genius for finance and was a hard man in a bargain. But he wanted more, much more, than he had. He had dreadful ambitions. And he had those fears of which I have spoken with regard to what the outside world thought of him; he was always correct to that outside world. For instance, he would dress me expensively for show purposes, but would perhaps deny me sufficient to eat."

"Mr. Barrett of Wimpole Street," I said almost to myself, but Gale caught the whisper.

"Oh no!" she answered quickly. "Mr. Barrett loved Elizabeth. It was a queer and perverse love, yes, but it was still love. My father had no feelings for me whatsoever. Apart from his almost ludicrous possessive attitude toward my brother, he was a human robot, an animated adding-machine."

"How soon did your stepmother enter the picture?" persevered Napoleon B.

"That's one of the damnable things, Mr. Smith. I was about six when my mother died, and I thought her a wonderful person. Of course, with the new baby motherless, there were nurses for him and a governess for me. I wanted to go to school like other children, but my father thought, I suppose, that this would remove me somewhat from his sadistic control and he kept me studying at home. Then, less than six, months after my mother died, my father brought my stepmother home. I was nearly beside myself. It seemed to me like the grossest sort of betrayal. You can be sure my father made the most of my young tragedy. But it wasn't long before I began to respect and then to love my new mother. She was one of the sweetest persons I have ever known." Here the girl's voice broke and she dabbed at her eyes, but our sympathetic silence soon restored her composure. "She had a refinement and culture that made my father's grossness seem even greater by comparison. I have often wondered what attraction my father had for the gentle woman who loved him. Jack possessed it in some measure, too. The attraction of opposites, I suppose, of a positive personality for a negative, although in the case of my brother it was his weakness that led my stepmother to attempt to shield and protect him from the force of the world. Do I make myself clear?"

"Painfully," I said, which wasn't what I had meant to say. It registered as badly as it sounded.

"Did your stepmother love your father?" Napoleon B. rescued me.

"Wildly! I think he was the first and last man she ever looked at. Of course, it's obvious to me now why he married her. He wanted her money. She had several hundred thousand dollars and a complete inexperience of life. Do you see why I hate money so? I hate it because my father did have a love that was part of his love of self. My father had the love of money."

"And it is the love of money that is the root of all evil," commented the fat man. "Go on."

"Well, as I say, I was soon drawn to my stepmother and she to me. While she was indulgent to the point of weakness with my brother, she reserved her intimacies for me. My heart, so starved for affection, was filled again. The inevitable happened. My father saw this. It made him furious to see me happy. But he waited, merely giving my brother more and more of what was denied me and making me hate my brother as I hated my father. Presently my father found out what his twisted soul wanted to know—that my stepmother was eccentric. She wasn't crazy, you understand, but her mind was so completely sensitive, she was so greatly introverted, she loved my father so undemandingly, that it needed only a mental blow to send her over the borderline into some milder form of insanity. My father set out to contrive that mental blow through us children, and particularly through me."

"Nice guy," I put in, chiefly to break the tension that was binding her and thickening her throat. She gave me one of her grateful smiles, and went on with less intensity.

"He sent me away to school. When I had wanted to go to school like a normal child, he had forbidden it; now that I had love and tenderness at home, he packed me off. He was a consummate sadist. My letters to my stepmother never reached her. Her letters to me came with decreasing regularity. They were letters that filled me with alarm; they were the letters of a woman who was not quite right. They spoke mutely of a woman retreating within herself. My father, it seemed, moved her into a separate wing of the house, and she could only see him by appointment, if you can imagine a marriage like that! If she had been a stronger woman, one more used to the ways of the world, she would probably have sought a divorce. Even the companionship of Jack was denied her . . . and he was growing up so spoiled and selfish, poor child, that his absence was better than his company. I know these things now, but then it seemed to me that the bottom had dropped out of my little world. Finally, my stepmother's pitiful letters ceased altogether. I have no doubt that she had retreated so far into her own existence that she had brought herself to forget mine."

"Then, for a long time you heard nothing from her?"

"No."

"Any idea what went on?"

"I can only guess, Mr. Smith. After my graduation I had sufficient confidence in myself to return home and face up to my father. He ignored me quite graciously, for I had ceased to be a factor in his life, except that he was obvious in his attempts from time to time to interest me in certain young men. They were always singularly dull young men, but astonishingly wealthy in their own right or heirs to great wealth. I was simply to be a magnet for him to attract more money and power. My brother Jack was by this time quite impossible. I simply couldn't stand him. He was sneaky and unreliable. I suspected him of inventing tales about me in order to create more trouble for me with my father. I caught him once stealing from my purse, and I gave him a sharp cuffing which taught him more respect for me. I see now, Mr. Smith, that it was really not his fault. By heredity and environment he was conditioned for the life he eventually led." She brought out her handkerchief again and held it briefly to her eyes. I took a quick gander at the thing and a bell clanged in my memory with a harsh sound.

"The greatest shock, of course, was my stepmother," she went on. "Gradually, I devoted my whole time to her welfare. In one way and another I pieced together what had happened. She had rapidly earned a reputation in the neighborhood for what is known when you are wealthy as eccentricity. My father saw that the legend was enriched. Then, when he had established with sufficient force to carry weight at law that my stepmother was presumably incapable of administering her own affairs, he struck! I can just imagine how he must have gloated when he told her that she would be committed unless she gave him an irrevocable power of attorney over everything she possessed. What was my poor, bewildered stepmother to do? Forced with the alternatives, she signed. Then he had no further use for her. He had her money with which to make the millions he craved, to achieve the power over others for which he lived. After that he almost forgot that she was alive. And yet, through it all, she continued to love him."

"'The ways of love are passing strange,'" Napoleon B. misquoted.

"As time went on, and with my continued company, my stepmother began to take some pitiful enjoyment from life. My father became aware of this and he set about to destroy her little measure of happiness. She had only two things— me and that stretch of semi-jungle she called her Green Mansions. Me, he could not touch. A brother of my mother's had died and left me a small fortune. I was completely independent of him and I defied him to try to send me away from my stepmother whom I had now grown to accept as one of two persons I genuinely cared for. My brother, of course, would have nothing to do with her. Well, my father did what might have been expected of a man of his temperament. He exercised his power of attorney and sold the land, including my stepmother's *Green Mansions*, for a golf course." She hesitated for a moment, then continued. "Mr. Smith, I suppose that by now you have read everything that can be read on the Cartwright family—if I remember your methods correctly from Mr. Allen's books."

Napoleon B. nodded gravely.

"Then no doubt you've read about my father's drowning?"

"Yes." The detective cleared his throat. "He fell overboard from his yacht."

"No," she said, "he did not fall. He was pushed!"

CHAPTER FIFTEEN

As the girl made her dramatic statement simply, Napoleon B. swore softly and feelingly. I knew it for a sign that the scent was strong.

"Pushed?" I asked, for want of something less of a cliché. "By who?" I was possessed with trivialities, as I often am at tight moments. "Or should it be, by whom? It wasn't *you*, was it?"

Her laugh was bitter. "Sometimes I wish I'd had that honor, Les. No, it was my stepmother."

"You're talking murder, Gale," said the large man.

"That's probably what the world would call it, Mr. Smith. That's why I've kept quiet so long. That's why I've shielded her, even though she's dead. Was I wrong?"

"I am not a judge, my dear, only a detective," he answered gently. "I would say you were wrong in not having told me this sooner. Your brother might still be alive; so might the policeman who died opening your mother's coffin. But these are only surmises on my part; I, too, may be wrong. I'm not infallible." It was quite an admission for him to make and I realized for the first time how strongly he was stirred by this girl's plight, how much his apparent brutality toward her was now revealed as the surest kindness. "Your stepmother would not have been held accountable by law," he concluded flatly.

"It was her own remorse from which I shielded her. You know, of course, that those who are mentally ill are not ill all the time. In all but the most severe cases there are varying periods of lucidity. My mother's case was one where she could be adjudged sane three-quarters of the time. In those sane periods she'd remember what she had done and reproach herself over and over again. A woman's love is a strange thing, Mr. Smith."

"So I've been told," said that confirmed bachelor.

"She would re-enact the scene in her tortured mind over and over again. She would see herself steal up behind him and push him with the strength of the possessed; watch him fall into the water, knowing he couldn't swim; laugh at him and taunt him as he thrashed around and cried for help; then, when he had gone, raising an alarm for him."

"And you saw her do it?"

"Oh, no! I did not go on that cruise. Nobody saw her do it. You see, they had a sort of private promenade off their cabin over the stern. It was a fancy of my father's. He was leaning over the rail and . . ." The girl shuddered at the invoked memory.

"Then how . . ."

"How did I know? It was very simple. In one of her lucid intervals Mother—I called her Mother by choice—told me. She had to tell someone. Obviously she could not tell Jack. He was a drunkard by this time and had been expelled from college for this and for other even more unpleasant practices. No, the only person she could tell was me. I made her see that she could accomplish nothing by making her act public.

I even confessed to her that I had felt like patricide many times. This seemed to cheer her up immensely. We never mentioned the subject again until about a week before her death. She had been growing more and more distrait. I asked her what was the trouble. She told me that Jack had finally wormed her secret out of her and was using it to blackmail her."

Napoleon B. whistled soundlessly. The picture was beginning to form for me, too.

"Nice lad," said the detective, "blackmailing his stepmother. What I can't understand, Miss Cartwright, is how your stepmother gained control of the Cartwright millions after your father's death. Surely her disability . . ."

"That's where father overreached himself, Mr. Smith. Like all unscrupulous men, he was too clever for himself. He considered himself good for many years. It sounds fantastic, I know, but my father never made a will. He died intestate, and control of the fortune fell to my stepmother again. She left the management of it, of course, entirely to Mr. Johnson."

"You mean Adam Johnson had her power of attorney?"

"Yes, mother trusted him implicitly. I believe he is a very good lawyer, is he not?"

"As shysters go, he's perfect. Well, it takes all kinds. What do *you* think happened to your stepmother, Miss Cartwright, remembering that we have no corpus delecti to prove that she died anything but a natural death?"

"I think," she answered slowly, "that mother, in one of her less lucid moments, threatened to tell everything. Jack saw himself exposed as a blackmailer. I do not believe it worried him about his stepmother being called a murderess. He knew that he was well-treated in her will. I think he killed her!"

It sounded too much like a Greek play. There must be a flaw in the dramatic perfection somewhere. Napoleon B. laid his finger on it.

"I don't believe," he said, "that Jack Cartwright had the nerve to kill anyone. Blackmail yes—he'd be right in style there. But murder—not that unlamented young man!" He slapped his hands on his knees as he rose. "You stay here, Gale, and rest. I'll see that a police guard is posted at your door. Not that it matters much. Unless I'm far off the mark, the attempts on your life are ended. In fact, the string is just about run out. We approach the Minotaur." He paused, fumbling absent-mindedly in his coat pocket with his un-bandaged hand. "There's only one thing that puzzles me about yourself. It's pretty hard to reconcile with everything else."

I knew what he was thinking; so did she.

"It's the handkerchief?" she asked.

He agreed.

"I can't understand that, Mr. Smith," she said earnestly. "I can't understand it at all. I had that handkerchief when I went out of the lawyer's office that afternoon. After that I lost it."

Something clicked with Napoleon B. Smith. I could see his little eyes snap with an idea, but all he said was, "There's another matter, Gale. It's personal and you don't have to answer it unless you want to. It may have absolutely no bearing on the case, and again it may, but I think I can get a solution without knowing. You said your stepmother was one of two persons you genuinely cared for. That other person, I take it, is Cyrus Handley."

Her eyes were wide and innocent. "Oh, dear, no, Mr. Smith." She laughed with unfeigned amusement. "I'm very, very fond of Cy. Perhaps some time, I don't know. When I said 'care for' I meant it in the sense of great affection for someone near and dear. The person I meant, Mr. Smith, is my stepmother's brother, Dr. Bryce."

I'll say this for Napoleon B. He didn't even blink!

"I understood," he said imperturbably, while, I looked my astonishment, "that Dr. Bryce was the family physician and an old and valued friend. I realized, when your mother made him executor of the will along with Mr. Johnson, that she held him in high esteem. But there has never been a hint of relationship, not even in the will. Why?"

"Two reasons. One is easy to understand if you know Dr. Bryce—his correctness, his dryness, his lack of a sense of humor. He did not wish to acknowledge my stepmother as his sister because he felt that his practice would suffer if his patient's thought there might be the taint of insanity, no matter how mild, in his family. You know how quickly a thing like that can ruin a doctor."

"It sure can," I contributed. "I remember a case where a doctor . . ."

"Yes, yes, Les," Napoleon B. interrupted me testily, "some other time. And the other reason, Gale?"

"The other reason is confidential, Mr. Smith and Mr. Allen. I would ask that you both keep it a confidence. My stepmother did not care to acknowledge Dr. Bryce. In many ways she was strict and old-fashioned. You see, gentlemen, there was a skeleton in the Bryce closet. Dr. Bryce was not my stepmother's natural brother."

I could see Napoleon B. pick up that piece, puzzle over it, try to fit it into the jigsaw, then shake his head figuratively and lay it down in his memory pile. The whole picture was blurred and out of focus, as I saw it. Nothing seemed to fit. There were too many disjointed angles, too few people to pin things on. Yet I knew that Napoleon B. Smith, by his very actions and words, by his assumed air of carelessness amounting almost to boredom, had found enough missing pieces to give him at least an inkling of the final result. He had a score or two of his own to settle!

"We'll respect your confidence," he said smoothly. "It seems to have no bearing at the moment. One more question about Dr. Bryce, then I'll go on to something else. Why was Dr. Bryce not at least hurt about being left out of the will? Your stepmother could have left him a substantial bequest without arousing too much curiosity. It's often done for family physicians who have looked after invalids or semi-invalids for years."

Gale reached for a box of cigarettes beside the table, but I anticipated her and she thanked me noncommittally. My hand trembled as I held the match, and I fancied I heard a faint chuckle from the fat man. She blew out a blue-white puff of smoke before answering.

"He *was* quite upset, as a matter of fact. He came to me in a tearing rage, saying that he had been cheated. I don't know what he meant, but he was making vague threats about having 'someone pay for this.' I presumed he meant to contest the will, but that would not be compatible with his nature, would it, to bring all that publicity upon himself and be forced to have his sister declared of unsound mind?"

"It certainly would not," agreed Napoleon B. emphatically. "His illegitimacy would inevitably come out in such a claim, and he would know how hard it is to break a will. No, it doesn't gibe. I suppose he was excited, but why?"

Gale exhaled smoke. I puffed nervously at my own cigarette. Napoleon B. coughed irritably; he hated cigarette smoke.

"Well, let's leave that for the moment," he answered his own question. "Now, about Cyrus Handley, my dear," The girl stiffened, but Napoleon B. went on, "You *are* in love with him, aren't you?"

"What if I am?" She was instantly belligerent, and as quickly apologetic. "Yes. I've promised myself to answer all your questions, no matter how silly or personal they may seem to me, because I feel you are the one person capable of ending this horrible mess. So I say yes, I do love Cyrus Handley. Is that so strange?"

"Oh, not by any means! A most engaging young man." He ignored my little snort of derision. "Handsome, talented, ambitious . . . very ambitious, isn't he?"

"Yes, very." Her voice had become eager. "His rifle and explosive business is building rapidly."

"He doesn't stand so well with Dun and Bradstreet's," the detective threw cold water.

'What do you mean?"

"His credit rating's all shot. I looked him up. He's been expanding too rapidly. Of course, now with that bequest from his aunt—your stepmother—he need have no further worries. That is, unless . . ." He checked himself. "By the way, Gale, has Cy Handley ever asked you to marry him?"

"Well, not exactly, but . . ."

"But you have hopes." She blushed. "Of course, you're not the heiress you once were. The shoe is on the other foot. Your stepcousin may be looking at things differently today."

The blush turned to a flush of anger. "Don't you think you're prying too far, Mr. Smith?"

"Perhaps I am, perhaps I am," he soothed. "It's the nature of my business, you understand. Makes me nosy."

We both laughed, and he seemed to forget about Cyrus Handley.

"We come to the last puzzling item, Miss Cartwright." The way he addressed her, familiarly one moment and formally the next, was typical. "That item is the matter of your inheritance."

The lovely girl deliberately crushed her cigarette in the ornate ash tray standing beside the bed, as Napoleon B. went on, "I shall quote from memory, my dear. Correct me if I'm wrong. In your stepmother's will it said, *for her faithful services, and for her many kindnesses to me in all but the one important instance of which she will be fully aware.* I repeat those last words, Gale . . . *of which she will be fully aware.* What was this one important instance?"

Gale Cartwright stood up and walked across and looked at herself in the mirror. What she saw did not please her, for she turned and made a face at Napoleon B.

"You do mark a lady up," she said flippantly.

"I asked you a question," he replied, and there was a lift of emphasis on the way he said "question."

Suddenly the poor kid began to cry, a heartbroken, tearing weeping. "I don't know," she sobbed, "I *really* don't know. I've thought and thought since it all happened but I can't think of one single thing. Mother always said she was leaving everything to me, but I paid no attention to that. I don't care about money for money's sake. But there was never any quarrel or anything between us, Mr. Smith, never anything but love. Please believe me!"

The large man went over and held her awkwardly, as men do who are not used to women. "There, there," he comforted, patting her on the shoulder with one of his ham-like hands, "it'll be all right. Everything's coming out. I *do* believe you. I only regret again that you didn't tell me all this before." He sighed. "But that's police work. Nobody ever trusts a policeman until it's too late."

He let her go, went over and picked up his hat, where he had let it fall to the floor. He gave me the get-out signal.

From the doorway he said, "Don't leave this room, no matter who wants you to, unless you have direct orders to do so from me. Whoever is responsible will know by this time that you must have decided to talk, if the papers are on the street with Perlotti's killing. I hope they've used that new cut of me you had made, Les," he added with some of his usual irrelevancy. "The other one made me look too old. Do you understand everything, Gale?"

"Y . . . yes, Mr. Smith." She was still sobbing a bit, but the sun was coming out. "I'll do exactly as you say."

"Then don't worry about a thing." He clapped his battered felt on his head. "It may interest you to know that I'm positive you've cracked this case. And I think I know where to find your mother's body, if it has not already been disposed of."

CHAPTER SIXTEEN

When we went down the stairs we were mobbed by reporters and photographers. Flashlights popped off from all angles. Napoleon B. Smith took it "big."

"Les," he once had said to me, "always play up to the press. The advertising it gives you on a case is dollars in your pocket for the future."

So he stuck out his chest and smiled all over his fat face, and asked if they wanted to shoot him from another direction. I wanted to shoot him, all right, but I didn't care about the direction.

The reporters were mainly interested in the Perlotti matter. One acute man from the *Mail's* police beat asked whether Napoleon B. was working on the Cartwright case, but the big detective parried that with a request that "you boys consider the Cartwright business off the record until I have time to give you the full information you need." While the "boys" nodded respectfully, for there is nothing more sacred to a newspaperman than something told him off the record, Napoleon B. saw Joe Brownlee glowering in the background, and added, "Of course, my capacity in the Cartwright case is purely unofficial. The man who has all the information is that sterling police official, Inspector Joseph Brownlee." In anybody else, it's ham!

It took us all of a half-hour to shake the reporters, and by that time Joe Brownlee was beaming. The world's best salesman of soft soap is Napoleon B. Smith. Joe hadn't had his picture in the paper for months. Now they snapped at least a dozen shots of him conferring with Napoleon B. The fact that the large man mugged all the pictures was lost upon the Inspector who was not adept at the art of publicity.

"Oh, by the way, Joe," said Napoleon B., when we had at last escaped, "I'd like you to do me a favor."

"Of course, of course," said the fly, rubbing his hands and walking into the parlor.

"I'd like to borrow a police car and a driver for today." The fat detective made it sound insignificant and commonplace. "Preferably Tim Curtis. That is, naturally, if you can spare 'em."

"Oh, naturally, naturally." Joe Brownlee rubbed predatory hands together. "Tim!"

Tim Curtis came over. He was a big, good-natured kid, with a marksman's certificate and an expert in judo. Quite a man to have on your side.

"I'd like you to go with Mr. Smith, Tim. Take the prowler. I'll go back to the station with one of the newspapermen." Tim saluted. "You're under Mr. Smith's orders, Curtis."

Of such is the kingdom of Napoleon B. Smith!

The first place we headed for was the morgue. I raised an eyebrow of inquiry at the detective, but he was preoccupied. It was restful letting a *good* driver operate for a-change. I relaxed and thought back over what Gale Cartwright had told us, and the more I thought the more puzzled I grew. Yet I knew that Napoleon B. had decided on a definite course of action.

When we arrived at the cheerless morgue building I started to get out with him, but Napoleon B. told me to stay put.

"I won't be more than a few minutes," he said.

He was gone about fifteen. However, Tim Curtis and I discovered a mutual interest in blondes, so I did not notice the time dragging particularly. Napoleon B. was noncommittal when he returned. I knew better than to try to drag anything out of him.

"Where's Rube Goldenberg hanging out lately, Tim?" he asked.

"They might know over at the *Five Aces Club*, Mr. Smith," the policeman answered respectfully.

"Okay, let's try it."

Still ignoring me, Napoleon B. lay back against the cushions, closed his eyes and clasped his hands over his paunch. I noticed he'd removed the bandage from his injured hand while in the morgue; it didn't look so bad to me.

Rube Goldenberg is quite a character. He's a weak, meek little man, with a penchant for two-dollar bets and bay rum and coke. I don't believe Rube has taken a bath of any kind since I've known him, and that's going on five years. Sometimes he shaves, but more often he'll let a beard grow and then lop it off with scissors. His nose runs continually and he wipes it on the sleeve of the coat he has been wearing for at least a decade. His eyes are red and rheumy, and his voice squeaks. Altogether he's someone you would rather stay away from.

But the Rube has ears—big ears for such a little man. Because he is so unkempt, nobody pays any attention to him

on the theory that he must be a half-wit at best. People say
things in front of the Rube they wouldn't confide to their
own mothers. As the Rube circulates amongst the criminal
element, this is readily understandable.

The Rube is the ears of Napoleon B. Smith, and his eyes,
too, when it comes to matters of the underworld. Napoleon
B. was brought up in a hard school. He learned early the lesson that "a good stoolie is worth ten thousand deductions."
Every police department uses these stool pigeons; they buy
immunity for their own petty crimes with the information
they give upon major robberies, gang murders and so on.
Napoleon B. had carried the Rube, and others less valuable, into his private detective practice. He admitted that
he could not function without them, and the Kohinoor was
the Rube. For money for his bay rum and parlays the Rube
would have turned in his entire family, assuming anybody
would ever own him as their own. It was his one joy in life;
the betrayal of his kind, the thrill of the hunt, the gnawing fear that he would sometime be discovered and put to
death slowly with an ice pick. Without the Rube and his ilk,
crimes unnumbered would go undetected.

Now, we did not just drive up to the *Five Aces Club*, a
dingy hole-in-the-wall poolroom, and ask for Rube Goldenberg. That would be like signing a death warrant. Instead, a
block or two from the place, Napoleon B. and I got out and
began to stroll. We knew the warning would be out of our
coming, but it made little difference.

We creaked down the filthy wooden stairs into the base-
ment where the click of pool balls came faintly from behind
the dirty-glassed door. As we reached the bottom, this door
flew open and a figure scuttled by us. Napoleon B. merely
reached out one hand and hauled the figure back, holding

him plenty far from both our noses. It was the Rube. This was a favorite act of ours. We would "arrest" him; he would protest; we would march him off somewhere for a heart-to-heart talk; presently he would return to his haunts, grinning because he had outsmarted the bulls, quite a hero in his own little realm, his ears glued to all conversations for our information and the gratification of his own peculiar lusts.

"Lemme go! Lemme go, you . . ." He rattled off a long string for the benefit of those listening on the other side of the door. "I ain't done nuffin'. Not a fing."

He was marched, still protesting, up the stairs. Curtis had driven up in the police car in the meantime. Anyone watching could see that it was a prowler. The Rube was thrown unceremoniously into the back seat and the car tore away from there in the manner of police cars the world over.

"The nearest station, Tim," growled Napoleon B., while the Rube sat up and grinned like a dirty fox, and I wondered if any would crawl on to me, for the detective had considerately placed me in the back seat with our captive.

Napoleon B. knew the sergeant on duty, and the sergeant let Napoleon B. and the Rube go off into a little room by themselves. I had beaten Tim Curtis two straight games of cribbage when the precious pair came out, their little confab over.

"Call me at my house at nine tonight," said Napoleon B.

"Sure fing," called back the Rube, already halfway out the door. He turned to screech derision at us in case someone might have tailed us, then vanished.

"The *Scarlet Pimpernel* in reverse," the fat man told us glumly. "Every time I see him I wonder whether he's real or if I'm just dreaming. No, no, Les, you counted that hand wrong. That should have been fifteen six and six is twelve, and you only counted ten."

"Muggins!" yelled Tim, grabbing the extra two points, which is what he beat me by. Life with Napoleon B. Smith can be difficult.

"I don't know what you need me for anyway," I said bitterly. "If you want to play secrets, why drag me along?"

He was contrite. "Get your hats and coats," he told us. "I want to get to the Handley Manufacturing Company, Incorporated, before it closes. And you can come in with me this time, Les."

'Thanks," I answered, but I knew the sarcasm was wasted.

Cyrus Handley was surprised to see us but he made us efficiently welcome. I could not help liking the man, even if Gale Cartwright was in love with him.

"I'm trying to find out if you've had any missing stock," Napoleon B. got right to the point, "such as T. N. T."

There was a frown deep between Handley's quiet, steady eyes. "I've been worried about that, Mr. Smith," he answered. "I've felt for some time that that missing stock, as you call it, was what was used to booby-trap my aunt's coffin. Have you learned any reason for that dastardly act?"

"Oh, several, several," conceded Napoleon B. genially. "Then you knew there was explosive missing?"

"Certainly! We check and double check on everything."

"Then why didn't you report it to the police?"

Handley resented the tone, that was evident, but he said graciously enough, "Because I felt reasonably certain as to who had taken the explosive. It was Jack Cartwright!"

That hit Napoleon B., I could see.

"Jack Cartwright! Why, he was . . ."

"Dead when the booby-trap was made. Yes, I know. It's very strange."

The fat man's face was a suety mask. "Do you mind telling me," he asked with elaborate casualness, "what your feelings are toward my client, Miss Gale Cartwright?"

Handley shot up from his chair, white with rage. Napoleon B. held up his hand apologetically.

"Never mind, never mind, Handley. That's answer enough." Handley sat down, mollified, only to start up again as the detective went on, "I hope you don't mind. I'm having you placed under arrest. Shall we call it protective custody, although, of course, there is no such thing legally?"

The young man seemed tensed for a spring.

"I wouldn't if I were you, Cy," said Napoleon B. mildly. "You're fast with a draw, I know, but you can't beat this ace up my sleeve."

It was the little gun he sometimes kept concealed up his arm, with a spring arrangement that shot it into his hand quicker than thinking. The wicked thing was staring one-eyed at Handley.

"If I don't do this," continued Napoleon B., "your life won't be worth insuring to last out the day. You've been double-crossed, my boy—double-crossed and triple-crossed."

With a hoarse cry, Handley flung himself at the door, but Tim Curtis tripped him neatly and put on a beauty of a hammer lock before Gale's stepcousin could regain his balance. Napoleon B. Smith merely smiled beatifically.

CHAPTER SEVENTEEN

"So he did it after all!" I said to Napoleon B.—not without a trace of malicious triumph—after Cyrus Handley, half-mad with anger, had been deposited bodily by Tim Curtis in the cooler.

"He did what?" asked the fat man mildly.

Napoleon B. said "Gin", and he had me again. Oh well, sometimes I'm lucky in love.

"Why, committed the murders, naturally!"

The detective had rustled a pail and some hot water and ammonia from somewhere in the station house, and had been soaking his big feet while we played gin rummy, although soaking his other end would have suited me better at the moment. Now he took one beefy mountain from where it was being slowly parboiled and held it up as far as his corporation would allow for purposes of critical examination. He grunted in earthy satisfaction and wiggled his toes comfortably. From his years on the beat he had flat feet, and now he babied his pedal extremities.

He was still studying his big toe when he answered me with, "Oh, Handley didn't commit any murders. At least, not that I know of. Didn't you hear me say I was taking him into protective custody? He feels like having my license now. Later on, when I explain things to him, I expect to be handsomely reimbursed. Handley's been a damn fool, but I wouldn't say he was a murderer, not on the evidence to date. But he'd have been a dead pigeon within twenty-four hours because he knows too much that he doesn't know he knows."

"Very clear!"

The big goof just grinned. He loves to rile me. He plunged the foot back into the steaming pail. I fancied I could hear the meat boiling. I know I was.

"Do you mean to say," I stormed at him, "that you've had young Curtis go out on a limb and jug Handley just to satisfy a whim of your own? Why, they'll break Tim just like that!"

"I'll cover for Tim. I never let anyone take the rap for me yet. The case is practically closed. You could see it as well as I do if only you used your eyes and your ears."

"Yeah!" I jeered. "Especially when you hog all the evidence to yourself. For instance, what was so interesting in the morgue today?"

"Bodies."

The big man ignored my enraged snort, moved his feet out onto the waiting towel, sighed in ecstasy. "Nothing like a foot bath after a hard day," he said to nobody in particular, meaning me. "I was looking at the old lady's body, of course."

That threw me.

"The old lady's body?"

"You usually look for a body in the morgue, don't you?" he asked coldly.

"Yes, but not *buried* bodies." I was beginning to feel punch-drunk. He hits me low like that on every case and I've never been able to call "foul" on him yet.

"This was an unburied buried body," he reminded me with unction. "Tell me, Les, if you had to hide a body, what better place to hide it than the morgue? Of course, you have to be able to get bodies into a morgue, but then if you're a resourceful murderer . . . This particular body was brought in by the police."

I ducked and rolled with the punch, not very successfully. I'm afraid I slammed my cards on the table in a manner unbecoming the gentleman that I am.

"The police?" I croaked.

"The police that took it away, of course." What I'd have given for the courage to push his fat face in! "Or had you forgotten our phony minions of the law? I have a great deal of respect for this murderer. Very daring. Sound strategy. Fooled me too long."

He did not know how close he was to having another murder on his hands, his own! He was occupied in drying his feet and I could easily have hit him and run, but I knew he'd catch me sometime.

"I keep telling you on case after case, Les," he lectured me, "that the hardest thing to dispose of in this world is a human body. It's practically impossible. Murderers have cut human bodies into little pieces and then been betrayed by those little pieces or by blood caught in drain traps. Murderers have sold human sausage meat and still been caught. Dental work, scars, tiny deformities, have all identified seemingly unidentifiable bodies, and phhht! there goes an alibi. No, Les, you don't *dispose* of a body; you get *rid* of it."

"But," I objected, running into the concealed left hook, "the old lady's body was already disposed of."

"My, my, what a memory!" He sighed ponderously and began pulling on his heavy wool socks which a doctor once told him he should wear for the sake of his feet. "Had you

forgotten we were going to exhume it? An autopsy was as
good as a death warrant from the murderer's point of view,
although I don't follow the murderer's reasoning on that. If
I'd been the murderer I'd just have sat tight, but I suppose
murder is a panicky thing firsthand. Anyway, the autopsy
on old Mrs. Cartwright is now being performed by the police surgeons. I'm waiting for the report, now." He tugged
at a recalcitrant right shoe. "I fear you'll never make a detective, Les."

"Well, I made *you*," I retorted hotly. "If it hadn't been for
my books, you'd still be peeking through keyholes."

"Oh, is that so!" This was the one subject on which I
could get Napoleon B's goat without half trying. "I'd like to
ask you, Mister Man, where your books would have been if
I hadn't provided you with the material by solving cases?"

We never get very far on this which-came-first-the-
chicken-or-the-egg argument. On this occasion we were interrupted by young Dr. Laird.

"It's as you thought, Napoleon B.," said the police sur-
geon, studying a slip of paper in his hand. "Mrs. Cartwright
was killed by a shot through the brain. I extracted the pellet
and Murphy had a look at it. He says it's a little outside his
ballistics experience, but as far as he can tell the bullet or
missile came from a high-powered air rifle. The old lady was
delicate and I believe the impact caused the bruise, making
it show more because there is little or no bleeding from a
wound of that nature."

An air rifle! Everywhere we turned in the case there was
an air rifle, except in the death of Jack Cartwright. At least
the murderer seemed to have varied the technique there.

The large detective grunted his thanks, taking the slip
of paper and stuffing it in his pocket without any seeming

interest. Dr. Laird seemed disappointed at this lack of reaction but I was used to it. I knew that when Napoleon B.
showed no excitement it was because something had happened that he had expected to happen.

"And still you clear Cy Handley?" I asked bitterly.

"I didn't clear him, Les. But I am not going to condemn
him solely because, among other things, he manufactures
air rifles. He could be the murderer. He could be an acces-
sory, before or after the fact. He could be an unwilling tool.
He could be completely innocent of any wrongdoing and
yet be inadvertently implicated. He could be entirely clear
of the whole affair. You pays your money and you takes your
choice, because it's all only a bet, on the evidence to date."

Confuseder and confuseder, as Alice would have said.

Napoleon B. hoisted himself to his feet. "Come on," he
said. "I've another visit I'd like to make. After what I've
been through it's rather a pleasant chore."

We picked up Tim Curtis and drove through the midafter-
noon traffic expertly. It was a treat to have Tim behind the
wheel. Besides, have you ever ridden in a police car and found
out how respectful automobiles and pedestrians can be?

"This guy Handley's talking big about getting my badge,"
said the young policeman nervously. "You sure everything's
okay, Napoleon B.?"

"I'll tell you what I'll do, Tim," answered the large man,
"and Les here is a witness. If things turn out badly—and
nothing can ever be guaranteed—I'll make it worth five grand
to you and see that you get a cop's job in another city. Okay?"

Tim's freckled grin was answer. Sometimes I think Napoleon B. Smith is the grandest guy on earth.

I hadn't heard where we were going. Presently we drove
up Montgomery Boulevard and stopped opposite the Federal

Building. The last time we'd been here was to see Dr. Bryce about the exhumation order. I raised an eyebrow at Napoleon B. and he nodded.

Dr. Bryce was pretty snappy. "I'm very busy today, Mr. Smith," he told us after the large man had persuaded a spectacular redhead in nurse's uniform to take in his card. "My office hours are just over and I was going to visit my patients."

"Your duties as coroner come first, Doctor."

"I don't need to be reminded of my duties, Napoleon B." Bryce hit back in the hectoring manner that made me dislike him so intensely.

"In this case I'm afraid you do." There was steel in the detective's voice, and for the first time a tiny frown of anxiety appeared between Dr. Bryce's eyes. "I would like to know why you iced the body of Margaret Jones in the morgue, and why you've just signed an order for release of the body, an order that, incidentally, will not be honored!"

One thing for which I had always given Dr. Bryce full marks was his ability to hang on to himself. But he really fell apart at Napoleon B's words. His jaw sagged like someone had just super-oiled the hinges. His little eyes bulged. His complexion turned from a nice, dignified parchment to a pale purple. He stared at us for the space of seconds, then he got up from his chair, pointed at the door with a finger that shook, and said, "G . . . g . . . get out!"

The fat man did not budge, and I took my cue from him. To say that I was enjoying myself is to speak slightingly of a Turner sunset. My only regret was that the scene was not taking place in an open court, for I could still feel the cut and smart of the coroner's sarcasm from that Cartwright inquest.

"Sit down!" Napoleon B. exploded the words, and I knew the time had come for action. "You made things very tough for me, unnecessarily tough, and I'd like to see you squirm for a while. Now, give on this Margaret Jones business or I'll call in the regular cops and hand the story to the press. You know how long you'll last in that pack of wolves."

"I tell you I don't know what you're talking about." Dr. Bryce had recovered his usual dry assurance. "I've never heard of this Margaret Jones."

"Perhaps you knew her originally as Mrs. Cartwright."

"Mrs. Cart . . ." Bryce stopped and his mouth snapped shut as though a spring had been released. Fear and puzzlement chased each other over his arid countenance.

"Yes, Mrs. Cartwright." Napoleon B. slipped a piece of paper out of his pocket. "Here is the order to the morgue, signed by you, instructing the attendants to hold the body of Margaret Jones for your disposition. How are you going to explain the fact that you placed in the morgue for safe-keeping a corpse that you knew to have been once buried and on whose inquest you sat as coroner?"

Dr. Bryce licked dry lips with a spittled tongue. His eyes darted from one of us to the other, as though unable to concentrate. I mentally applied for permission to adjust the rope, being vindictive and amoral where my vanity has been severely wounded.

"I . . . I don't understand," he stammered. He drew the back of his hand over a coldly-damp forehead. "Really . . . really, it's all very . . . strange. Quite strange. I . . . I . . ."

The physician collapsed onto his chair, swinging wildly from side to side as the swivel seat rocked. His eyes rolled back in their sockets. Napoleon B. Smith leaped for him, tugging at his collar and yelling at me to call the nurse, which was no hardship for me. This redhead would have brought any man out of a faint just by walking into a room—any man, that is, other than Dr. Bryce. For him it took brandy. This family certainly went in for faints at the psychological moments.

"For . . . forgive me," he spluttered finally, looking again more like old saddle leather than a freshly laundered pillow slip. "You . . . you shocked me so I . . . I quite lost my senses. I believe you spoke about an . . . an order . . . one, signed by myself. Might I . . . would you be good enough . . . could I see it?"

I must say that Dr. Bryce was more human at that moment than he had ever seemed to me. In fact, he looked like a tired, bewildered old man who had carried a burden for too long and now wanted to shrug it from his shoulders. While the nurse gently held his head and I was wishing I had had sense enough to faint, Dr. Bryce looked at us pathetically from the white-enameled examining table where we had laid him.

As though coming to a decision that was hard to make, Napoleon B. said, "I'll hold the order in front of you, Doctor. You'll understand why I can't allow it in your hands."

A thin and quickly vanishing smile ran across the coroner's lips. He nodded, and the fat man held the piece of paper delicately between both thumbs and forefingers, almost blocking the view. Realizing this, he sheepishly took the slip by his fingernails. Sometimes Napoleon B. Smith is unhappily conscious of his bigness, but not often.

Dr. Bryce studied the order as though his life depended on it. Then he said, "It's a very good forgery."

All the ego ran out of the detective. It was his turn to play loose-mouth. "Forgery?"

"It must be a forgery," returned the coroner with reasonable calm, considering the circumstances. "I didn't sign it, and if you do not sign your own name that is what is called in law a forgery."

"Very funny," growled Napoleon B., completely discomfited. The large man thought a moment, then picked up one of the prescription pads. "Copy it then," he commanded. "If it's a forgery, you won't be afraid. You know I can prove beyond a reasonable doubt whether it is a forgery or not, but that takes time. Right now, time is the least thing we have. I'd like a comparison."

The coroner wrote swiftly, while the nurse ran her fingers along his temples in a way that gave me goose-pimples. It was a waste of talent. Even with the pad propped up on the doctor's knee it was plain to see he was making no attempt to disguise his handwriting. After a final flourish he handed the pad to the detective without a word. Napoleon B. studied both scripts earnestly. There was an uncomfortable silence in the consulting room. Bryce knew his entire career, perhaps his life, hung on the next few moments.

Napoleon B. looked the doctor full in the eye at last. "I'd give an amateur opinion," he said, "that it is a forgery. I'll give a professional guess that the forgery was done by an expert, somebody like Harry the Pen. Okay, Doc, I'll hand you a clean bill of health."

The way he said it, I didn't know whether he meant it or whether it was just a stall. I could see the coroner felt the same way about it.

CHAPTER EIGHTEEN

Napoleon B. Smith was gloomy as he hunched himself in the chair in our living room. I did not question, but I thought I knew the trouble. He had been certain Dr. Bryce was the murderer; now he was not so sure. He could not eliminate the coroner, but neither could he tip off Inspector Brownlee to have him arrested. If he was wrong, Bryce could sue him for more money than the detective would make in a lifetime.

Detective work is like any other kind of work; it has its discouragements. Perhaps its disappointments are even more terrifying than in other jobs for, on the success or failure of a detective, human lives and hopes and miseries are bound. And it is, at best, a solitary occupation, much like that of a writer, where a man does not like to speak his mind to another for fear of error and possible later ridicule. I have seen Napoleon B. so anguished with the snarls of a case that he has left a dish of ice cream all but untouched. Similarly when I get to a high point in a story and I think I have everything straightened out, all of a sudden the ending looks incredible and I sit staring at a blank page for an hour or two, unable to write a word.

From where I sat, the entire thing was a rigamarole. An old lady is murdered. Her stepson is given the bump. Her stepdaughter knows the old lady has committed murder, no matter what you want to call it morally. An underworld hood tries to punctuate the girl's life period. The old lady's body is spirited out of her tomb by some phony policemen who seem to have vanished. The casket blows up because it's been booby-trapped, hoping to catch Napoleon B. The old lady's nephew manufactures air rifles, and an air rifle killed the old lady and nearly got the stepdaughter. The said nephew is now in so-called "protective custody," sounding more like Gestapo stuff to me. The coroner on the old lady's case is revealed to be her illegitimate brother and one of the executors of her will, along with her lawyer. The old lady's body is found in the morgue where it has been consigned on an order the coroner claims is forged. If we'd had a butler, I'd have rung for aspirin.

I knew what we were waiting for—the call from Rube Goldenberg. I could almost feel how much Napoleon B. was depending on that call to straighten him out. It was about seven-thirty. Rube was told to call at nine, and he's as punctual as an electric clock. I tried to work on my book without much success. Nothing can be as slow as Time.

At eight-fifteen the telephone rang. Napoleon B. let it ring twice, he was so surprised. Then he lifted the receiver warily. I could hear the Rube's voice clearly; it had a whispery carrying power.

"Mr. Smiff," he said. "I gotta see ya right away. I got somefing importan' fer ya. I'm up at Jake's Place, Room Free Oh Five."

"Listen, Rube!" Napoleon B. spoke tensely. "What's the gag? I told you to . . ."

There was a click at the other end. Napoleon B. replaced the receiver in its cradle, puzzled. He sat thinking for a full minute, ignoring me completely. Then he seemed to come to a decision. He dialed a number, asked for Tim Curtis, and told him to pick us up just as fast as he could without using his siren. After that the large man heaved himself up, went to a desk, and took out an automatic which he tossed to me. I caught it indignantly; he knows I'm a dub with firearms and likes to torment me with them.

"Better slip the safety catch off," he interrupted my splutterings mildly. "I've a hunch you're going to need that little friend tonight."

"Why would the Rube call you before nine o'clock?" I asked.

"Exactly what *I'd* like to know." There was indecision and discouragement in the large man's voice, and it worried me. When a monumental egotist starts to fumble, it's time for lesser folk to duck what he's juggling with. "You don't have to come on this, Les, unless you want to. It's going to be plenty dangerous."

The big rhino! He can get around me every time.

It wasn't long before there was the sound of tires crunching on the gravel of the driveway, and a horn honked. Napoleon B. was telephoning, and I went to the door and called out to Tim that we'd be right out, so I missed what the detective was saying. The large man looked happier when he joined us.

Jake's place is the most unsavory joint in the whole city, a tenth-rate hotel with a clientele made up exclusively of underworld characters who don't want to be bothered. The police leave it alone, except for an occasional raid, because they'd rather know where to put their fingers on someone when that someone has pulled a job and left his trademark. The way Napoleon B. has explained it to me, every con man or crook has his or her own way of working. A swindler will pull the same con game with variations wherever he goes. A pete man will blow a safe to the same pattern time after time. Habit has caught more criminals than fingerprints. You can remember to wear gloves, but breaking a chain of habits is something else again. The smart copper can tell you, just by looking at a job, whether it's pro or amateur, and, if he has one of those mental rogues' galleries all good policemen should have and it's a pro pull, I'll give odds he can name the mug responsible or at least two or three who have been trained in the same school. So, when you wonder why the police don't move in and clean out a place like Jake's, just remember that until the millenium such joints are handier than a fire extinguisher when the blaze is small.

We parked the police car two blocks away, and Napoleon B. said Tim could come with us because he was in plain clothes. He told him to walk about twenty feet in the rear of us and to keep his eyes on what might go on behind.

"You'd better keep your artillery handy," he told us, "but don't get trigger-happy. This case has been buggered enough already."

The narrow, filthy street seemed to reach out to us with foul-smelling hands: The air was tangible with stealth. We walked lightly on the balls of our feet, and, while we seemed to look ahead and not to care, our eyes were trailing corners. The sweat came under my armpits the way it does when I'm excited, and it trickled coldly down my sides. Tim's thudding brogans were unnecessarily loud behind, us, despite the fact that the street and the leaning houses around were full of noises and screams and children ferreting in garbage cans and leaning out of windows to yell obscenities at us.

I wondered why the trail of the murder of the little old lady was leading from the eternal green twilight of *Hell's Half-Acre* to the noisome man-made jungles of this polluted heart of the city.

The door to Jake's Place leaned tipsily on broken hinges towards the street, while the gloom of the interior was barely dispelled by an anaemic, fly-specked light bulb suspended far up the wall. Napoleon B. brought out his flashlight and played it around, but nobody showed. Inside was a dingy door with a barely discernible "Office" painted on it. Rickety stairs led steeply to landings that went on and on into repellent darkness. The place seemed deserted, yet we knew that in all that old and loathsome building eyes were watching and ears were listening and fingers were uneasy on triggers. Tim came up and stood behind us, a comfortable bulk in the unreality of our surroundings. I wondered how human beings could live here, and then I remembered Rube Goldenberg and he was not a human being. I recalled what man has done to man, and how great criminals ride in Rolls Royces and little crooks skulk in holes like Jake's Place, and how the viciousness of a life like this is the result of the indifference of those who have power and who go to fashionable churches and collect their rents from tenements and brothels and the hideouts of those whom they have placed beyond the law. I knew that the murderer we sought came from that upper stratum and had not been above seeking the help of those who, unlike himself or herself, had not had the opportunity to keep above the level of Jake's Place.

"Rube was trying hard to tip me to something," Napoleon B. was saying in my ear. "I don't know what, but be ready for whatever happens."

He gave a quiet signal to Tim, switched off the flash, and led us in a tiptoe assault on the stairs. It seemed to my heightened imagination that they cracked like pistol shots under our several weights.

At the second landing Napoleon B. leaned over to whisper to Tim. "You stay here. Give us five minutes. You a watch?" He grunted, pleased when the young policeman showed him a luminous dial. "You'll do, kid! If I don't send Les down for you in five minutes from now . . . no, make it six . . . you come a'shooting. Check?" Tim nodded. Napoleon B. and I started up for the third floor.

It seemed lonelier without the feel of Tim Curtis behind us. There had been feeble lights on each of the first two landings, but the third was pitch black. Even the large man was affected. His breathing came to me spasmodically. He seemed to feel out each step with a mastodonian foot, letting each large boot down as softly as a child's kiss. I made myself as much his noiseless shadow as possible. There had been twenty-three steps to each of the other flights. I counted desperately as we mounted. It must have taken us less than a minute, yet it seemed at least an hour.

Jake's Place seldom had an empty room, yet it was quieter than Mrs. Cartwright's tomb before the explosion, and had something of the same quality of dead air and unalive expectancy. It emanated evil. Perhaps I was hypersensitive because of Napoleon's warning, but I fancied ghostly chuckles and hidden, obscene laughter coming from behind those closed, blank doors we had gassed.

As we came to the top of the stairs, a door along the hall opened softly, and we both stiffened.

"Don't show a light'!" pleaded Rube's whiny voice. "I'm the fourf door along on the lef'. Jus' take it easy." His whispers carried to us, but no further.

We felt our way down the hall, the detective counting the doors by touch, and I hanging on to his coattails. After a while he paused. The blackness ahead, a trifle grayer, filtered through a filthy window.

"In here," said the Rube, and there was such urgency in his tone that my spine tingled.

I could feel the large mass in front of me move and I followed blindly. Then I heard Napoleon B. breathing freely for the first time in minutes. It made my own heart less pitty-patty. A door closed behind us.

"Okay, Rube," said Napoleon B. jovially. "If you've a light in here turn it on and let's get down to business."

A light came on—a blinding beam of a three-cell torch! It came full into our eyes.

"Welcome to the party, Napoleon B.," said a voice behind the flashlight, a voice evidently muffled by some kind of a mask. "And I wouldn't try a thing. I'm carrying an automatic rifle, and I needn't tell you what a mess it would make of things in this small space, including, of course, yourselves." The voice was tantalizingly familiar for all its disguise. We had not moved from where the light had rooted us. "If you please, my friend, will you kindly do the honors?"

Rube Goldenberg shuffled and snuffled into the beam of light, but not in the direct line of fire, carrying several lengths of rope. What was intended for an apologetic look gave him a very hangdog appearance. He wiped his nose nervously on some of the handy rope, then came up behind the detective.

"Put your hands behind your back, fat man," sneered the voice. Napoleon B. hates any direct reference to his avoirdupois.

"One, two, three, it's all the same to me," said the detective mockingly, but I knew the score. He was telling me three minutes had gone.

"Shut up!" snarled the voice. "Get busy, you!"

The "you" in the shapeless shape of Rube Goldenberg began tying us up, and making a good job of it, too.

"I couldn't help it, boss," he whined and snuffed loudly. "It was me or youse."

"You're a lousy rat, Rube," said Napoleon B. genially enough, "but then I never did have any respect for your ability."

"Tie those knots tighter," called the voice. "I'm watching."

"I suppose you know you won't get away with it," the large man spoke easily.

For a moment, there was an uneasy silence. Then the voice said, "If I don't, you won't be around to celebrate." Which was certainly a comfort!

"You underestimated me, Napoleon B.," said the voice.

"I'm afraid I did."

It was apparent to me what the detective was doing. He was stalling for time.

"You underestimated me, both as to my mental and physical resources." A sneering chuckle slid the distance between us, leaving me shivering with its malignancy. "I did not make the mistake of underestimating you. I gauged every move correctly. When my . . . ah . . . underworld acquaintances informed me that your stool pigeon here was making discreet inquiries about me, I knew exactly how to handle the situation. You walked straight into my trap."

Time walked by on slow feet. Half seconds crawled into seconds. The bonds about my wrists started to cut off circulation. The voice of the murderer was inflaming me with fear.

"You'll not leave here alive. And for the trouble you've caused me I've devised a singularly unpleasant death." Now I knew! The murderer might not be mad, but the murderer was a sadist and a megalomaniac. Every action and word shouted of these. "Back up here to me, Goldenberg!"

The Rube cringed toward him. Even in the blinding glare of the flashlight, I could see his dirty and seamed face working in an unholy terror. A gloved hand flipped a noose around him, drew it tight, threw him violently against the wall behind us. The beam of light worked around towards the door. I had been counting what I thought were seconds, but they had the leadenness of eternities.

The floor creaked under the murderer's backward steps. There was the rattling of a can.

"Five gallons of gas coming up!" the voice chuckled, and the horror grew.

The murderer seemed to be fumbling with one hand while keeping the flashlight trained on us. I knew the automatic rifle was probably in the crook of his working arm. There was the gurgle of a liquid running into an open can.

"Here's a bath for you all. It'll be a surprise to the Rube."

"Wait!" screamed the stoolie. "I helped you."

"This is the triple cross, Rube."

Bright liquid arced through the air, sloshing against us. Gas fumes choked us. Running into our eyes, soaking through our clothes, the loathsome fluid blistered intolerably as it reached the more tender portions of our skin and bodies. I writhed in agony. Napoleon B. made a futile lunge. The murderer backed to the door, while the gasoline ate at us with a gnawing. There was insane laughter as the murderer opened the door preparatory to backing out.

"Burnt men tell no tales!" said the murderer. "When I throw a lighted match, you'll have hell before you get there, and I'll be down the fire escape and away. You'll never be recognized."

"There'll be an explosion," Napoleon B. said grittily. "You'll be caught yourself."

It made the murderer pause, as something to which no thought had been given. I fought against the wave of nausea that was trying to wash me into merciful oblivion. It's strange how we cling to life, the thing we seldom value until it is to be snatched from us. Then the murderer obviously made a decision, chancing possible destruction for the surety of wiping out all evidence. He fumbled for a match! One last taunt was flung at Napoleon B. Smith.

"Yes, sir, you walked right into it, and no way out, Napoleon B."

The detective spoke through teeth clenched to keep back his cries. "Maybe you're right. But if I were standing behind you right now, I wouldn't give you the satisfaction of shooting you. I'd slug hell out of you!"

Tim Curtis took the hint. He reversed his service revolver, and brought the butt crashing down on the murderer's skull. That much I saw before the pain got the better of me.

Air, blessed air, revived me. In minutes, I could distinguish outlines. There was no mistaking Tim Curtis and Inspector Joe Brownlee.

"You'll get a promotion, kid," I whispered, but I couldn't grin. I was a mass of bandages. Gasoline blisters like hell. Tim just knocked one foot against the other bashfully.

"You all need your heads read," said the Inspector wrathfully. "I tried to talk Napoleon B. into letting us handle this, but he said he wanted the satisfaction of laying the murderer by the heels himself. Well, you mugs got satisfaction all right!"

There was the clang of the ambulance bell. Two internes fell out of the rear with a stretcher. The street was starting to revolve slowly.

"How . . . how is the big lug?" I asked.

"He's had some of his fat fried, that's all." Joe was still angry, but it was wearing off quickly. He turned to Napoleon B. where he lay about ten feet from me, first-aided in the same way. "Oh, all right, you big stiff, you broke the case. I've been so busy I haven't even had time to take a peek at the murderer."

Napoleon B. waved a weak but magnanimous hand. "It's your case from now on, Joe. Take off the mask yourself." The detective tried to grin and failed. "Like I said before, you take the credit. All I want is the cash."

Inspector Brownlee hesitated, then walked over to a very still black-clad figure lying half-covered with a friendly blanket. There was no telling whether it was a man or a woman, or even human. The head was completely concealed by a black stocking-cap.

"Whoever it is really went in for melodrama," the Inspector said, looking down and shaking his head.

"Progressive," answered the detective, motioning away the bored internes. "A couple more killings and the killer would have been certifiable. Go ahead, tug the damn thing off. I'm not interested. I know who it is, anyway."

In spite of the fact that I wanted nothing more than clean sheets in a hospital with a pretty nurse to take my pulse, I managed enough strength to sneer at him, "If you're so smart, tell us who it is before Joe yanks off the mask."

"Fair enough," agreed the fat man. "It's Adam Johnson."

It was, too.

CHAPTER NINETEEN

Gale Cartwright came to see me in the hospital, wearing a handsomer-than-ever Cy Handley decoratively on her right arm. They exclaimed over the mess that the gasoline had made of me, but I told them that wasn't the half of it, that we'd almost had three on a match. The girl laughed when I told her how Rube had been so dirty he'd scarcely blistered at all; that all the gasoline had done was wash him clean. But I could see that in the back of their eyes there was pain and gratitude mixed and a hint of something else that spelt future contentment.

"Why aren't you and Napoleon B. in the same room?" Gale asked.

"The walrus has such a colossal vanity," I told her, "that he wouldn't let even me see him in his present condition. For a guy who could double for Gargantua, he's really a percy-pants."

I didn't mean it, of course. I was sore because I couldn't talk to Napoleon B. about the case. Apparently he'd clammed up with everyone. All I knew was what I had had read to me in the papers by my nurse, who was so much of a gargoyle I suffered a relapse every time I saw her.

"Mr. Smith is a very strange character," said Gale with a sigh.

"He's a character, period!" I hated wasting what few words my chopped steak lips would let me speak on that overblown mass of blubber. "And thanks for the posies."

She blushed prettily over that.

"I could cheerfully have torn Mr. Smith apart," Cy Handley put in his two cents' worth, "when he had me man-handled into jail. Now I realize I owe him my life."

"You'll get a bill for it." I was definitely sour. I hate a guy with dimples—dimples can beat my time without half trying. "He probably will overvalue it."

They both thought I was being funny.

Dr. Bryce was a visitor, too. You could have knocked me over with Joe Louis' Sunday punch when he came in the door. I was getting used to surprises. But Baby Snooks could have floored me cold for what came in with him, namely and to wit, his redheaded nurse. My doctor had to put me back on a soft diet because my temperature went up; what can you expect when a fever-arouser lays a cool hand on your forehead and coos at you?

"Now that things are cleared up," said the coroner, "I must apologize to you. I am afraid my manner is not . . . ah . . . always conducive to cordial relations."

I waved a swaddled hand. "That's all right, Doc. Forget it! For what you've done for me this afternoon, I could forgive you if you'd bumped Napoleon B."

He didn't get it, so I let it lay. But the redhead gave me laughter sparks from her green eyes. *She* got it. Oh, doctor!

Over and over again, I told myself, "That was Adam Johnson you saw when Brownlee yanked off the mask," but I couldn't put the jigsaw together. I knew I had most of the pieces, but a big fat goof who wanted to pretty up his ugly pan was the only person who could fit in the missing parts to my satisfaction. Besides I was getting lonesome for him, not having seen him for nearly a whole week.

My recovery was alternately helped and retarded by Marjorie. Marjorie? Dr. Bryce's titian-tressed office come-on. She visited me three times in the next ten days. I was almost afraid to have them take off the bandages. The shock might kill the delicate plant of our romance.

It was another hot day as Napoleon B. Smith and I stood at the first tee of the Briar Hill course. The detective shrieked to everyone, through the medium of his Joseph-colored sweater, that he was a golfer. It was a garment from which no eye could hide. There was quite a lineup at the first tee; it was a Saturday morning and Napoleon B. and I had followed doctor's orders and had slept late.

"You and Mr. Allen are number twelve, Mr. Smith," said the starter. "I'll call your number."

"You'll find us at the nineteenth hole, Tom," answered the fat man expansively. "Have one of our caddies call us."

It was our first morning after convalescence and it had been a day that practically begged for the royal and ancient game. I had not yet had more than snatches of talk with Napoleon B., and I was burned up with curiosity. But I knew better than to hurry the maestro; he would tell all when he saw fit, and not before.

Over a tall, cool one, with a small collar, I watched the fat man spoon into a tutti-frutti sundae, with a chocolate marshmallow standing by for a chaser.

"You train like that," I told him in mild disgust, "and you'll not last nine holes, much less eighteen."

The little eyes twinkled at me with rare good humor.

"Listen to who's talking!" His spoon made motions at my glass. "Don't tell me ice cream isn't better for you than that stuff."

He had me there. He always has an answer.

"Well," I changed the subject about as adroitly as an amateur changing reels for the first time on a 16-mm. projector, "the Cartwright case is closed and, as the *Mail* put it so originally, 'it was certainly a feather in the cap of Inspector Joseph Brownlee.'"

Napoleon B. grinned wolfishly. He finished off the tutti-frutti delicately, shoved it aside, and began attack on the other goo. "What do I care, Les? Credit does him some good. Cash salves all my wounded feelings, my professional pride, or anything you care to name."

I regarded him with loathing. "Some day you'll cut my throat for money."

"I never charge for entertainment." He was enjoying himself so much it was a crime. He paused for a moment, then, "It was all so absurdly simple."

That untethered my nanny. "Cut the alleged comedy," I told him sharply. "You know damn well it was a difficult case and that your brain work was exceeded only by your confounded luck."

The large man laughed good-naturedly.

"I know how you figured the old lady wasn't killed by your golf ball," I went on, "but what I can't figure out is why Johnson changed his original plans."

"Panic." A large hunk of ice cream slid down the waiting cavern. "Pure panic. Traps more murderers than enough. Here was a practically faultless plan. In fact, I'll go further and say it was almost the perfect crime we always talk about." He looked at me soberly. "Yet there can be no such thing as a perfect crime, Les. I'm far from a religions man, as you know, but someone was watching. Something aided my golf ball into that old lady's *Green Mansions* at the particular moment of that particular day. Do you believe that?"

I shrugged. You don't explain the inexplicable.

"Otherwise, the old lady's death is declared accidental, our murderer's still a reasonably respected citizen, and who's to give him away?"

"Nobody."

Napoleon B. shook his ponderous head. He was enjoying himself like an actor taking curtain calls after an especially good performance.

"Oh yes there is—the weak link in the otherwise strong chain, the piece that clicks the Chinese puzzle into place, or should have, anyway, if I'd been feeling up to par. The second mistake. The first mistake," he added modestly, "was pure accident—my discovery of the body. If it had been anybody else but me, he might have got away with it."

Let him brag! He had delivered the goods, so give him sounding cymbals! Do not remind him of a coroner's jury verdict or of his own grief at the thought that he had killed a harmless old lady.

"The second mistake," the detective went on complacently, "was using Jack Cartwright as a tool. But then, there couldn't have been any murder without Jack Cartwright, could there?"

I lead him on with, "In what way?"

"Well, we know that the so-and-so was blackmailing his own stepmother. He had found out about her murdering his father, and he was using the knowledge to extract money from her. But a blackmailer is never satisfied with small pickings, particularly an incurable spendthrift like Jack. On pure guesswork I'd say the old lady probably got stubborn and refused to kick through with the large amounts he now wanted. He began to borrow money from Cyrus Handley. Then Handley began to squeeze, because Handley himself was squeezed because of the expanding of his business. Jack found himself stuck. Still theorizing, the old lady must have gone to Adam Johnson with her problem. Remember that Gale Cartwright said her stepmother trusted the lawyer implicitly. We trust the strangest persons in our lifetimes!"

"How true!" I murmured, but he missed it.

"Adam Johnson probably offered to loan Jack Cartwright the money he needed to pay back Cy Handley. Handley tells me that by that time he was threatening to go to Jack's stepmother. Cy is a business man first, a philanthropist 'way down the list. I would say that Jack, weak and vicious as he was, soon fell under the sway of the crafty lawyer. The stepson might even have been the one to conceive the notion of murdering his own stepmother. I am inclined to think he was, and then Adam Johnson saw it as the way out of insuperable difficulties." The detective sighed heavily. "But once the deed was done, once the stepmother was out of the way, Johnson realized the greatest menace to his safety was the weak, drunkard stepson. The first decision to murder must have come hard. The second was easier. Jack Cartwright had to be eliminated."

I sipped my beer thoughtfully, and Napoleon B. seized the opportunity to demolish the last of the ice cream. The whole story was macabre to the nth degree.

"Wait a moment!" I said. "I'm still not clear on how you discovered exactly how the old lady was killed."

The fat man chuckled obscenely. "Elementary, my dear Watson!" He liked to compare me to Watson because it made him feel like Holmes. "All that's necessary to figure out things like that is to be a great detective."

The lucky bum!

CHAPTER TWENTY

When I saw that Napoleon B. was trying to attract the steward's eye, I cut in on him hastily. If he ate any more ice-cream his head would start coming to a point and he'd be giving me a frozen stare.

"You and Philo Vance!" I jeered, to bring his mind back to his work. "If you fell in poison ivy you'd come up covered with four-leafed clovers."

"All right, I'll admit something. *I didn't know exactly* how the old lady was killed—until Adam Johnson made his confession. But I had a good idea. Good ideas aren't evidence, however," he smirked. "You can call it luck if you want, but I had so much actual evidence against Johnson that admitting the killing of Mrs. Cartwright could add nothing more to his sentence. In the first place, three of us can accuse him of attempted murder, mayhem, felonious assault and what have you. That's good for life imprisonment, or the equivalent for a man of his age and physical condition. We can prove he hired Perlotti to do away with Gale Cartwright. He is directly implicated in the murder of Jack Cartwright. He's a smart lawyer in his own right, and he's hired Simons who is even smarter, and I imagine his confession will be ruled out as soon as the trial gets under way. So it has to be sewn up a dozen different ways to make sure of him."

"Let's begin at the beginning," I said, resolved to keep him as much on the rails as possible. "I know from Johnson's confession that he needed to cover-up defalcations from the Cartwright estate that ran into six figures and that he needed money to pay off gambling debts. That much is clear. But what put you on his track in the first place?"

"Well, I must admit that my prime suspect was Dr. Bryce. He had motive, opportunity, everything that goes to make a good murderer. When my case against him collapsed over that forgery, there was only one other logical suspect."

"Why? I agree that Dr. Bryce had plenty of motive, and his opportunity for murdering Jack Cartwright was there, all right. But *where* was his opportunity to murder old lady Cartwright?"

"Think back to the layout of the Briar Hill course. You know that because of the dog-leg seventh hole, the sixth and seventh fairways are practically parallel, at least for the first leg of the seventh, with *Hell's Half-Acre* running down the middle. Now, remember that the body was warm, quite warm, when we reached it. The golf course was not crowded that morning, but strangers are always noticed wandering around without clubs. What does that suggest?"

"Well, I'd say that the old lady must have been killed just before we got there, and that the murderer must have been a golfer, otherwise he would have attracted attention."

"Precisely. Now, we both know there was a foursome following us because we sent back for Dr. Bryce when the old lady's body was discovered. At the time we thought nothing more of the following foursome. But when I considered the topography of the course in conjunction with the opportunity for murder, the murderer *had* to be amongst that foursome! Check?"

"I suppose so."

"You *know* so. Anyway, I checked with the starter on that foursome. It was composed of Dr. Bryce, Tony Pearson, Jock Crandall and Adam Johnson. Pearson and Crandall appeared to have not the remotest connection with the case, but I had them looked into for safety's sake. As I assumed, they were only slight acquaintances of the Cartwright family. That left Adam Johnson and Dr. Bryce as the possible murderers. Bryce seemed to be the man, especially when I weighed his actions against my later knowledge. Almost from the first, therefore, I had only two suspects."

I thought back over some aspects of the case. "With only two suspects, you certainly kicked others around plenty."

"But there again you don't look any farther than that protuberant proboscis. If you put yourself in my shoes . . ."

"No thanks!"

". . . you look at things a little differently. Conceding that only Bryce or Johnson could be the murderer of Mrs. Cartwright, the circle of suspects widens to include Gale Cartwright and Cyrus Handley when the murder of Jack Cartwright is considered. In other words, I must enlarge my theory to consider the possibilities of a plot involving two or more of the suspects."

He paused to let the point sink, and then went on. "Let me skip a bit to make Johnson's motives clear for your infantile mind. Or rather, let's consider motives. Dr. Bryce is a dry old stick with a skeleton in his closet—he would kill to keep it under lock and key. Cy Handley needs a lot of money in a hurry and it's there for him in the old lady's will. Gale, we were told in the will, had been kind to old

Mrs. Cartwright 'in all but the one important instance of which she will be fully aware.' Gale could have killed her stepmother or her brother for revenge. Even if we eliminate her from the stepmother's death on the grounds that she was not a golfer there is still the important evidence of her handkerchief dropped in Jack's apartment. You agree that these are all legitimate reasons for murder?"

"Men have been killed for less."

"Much less. But we have no motive for Adam Johnson. It is a missing motive. I never eliminate missing motives because a motive may turn up in the most unexpected places at the most curious times. Rube Goldenberg furnished me with the key that almost cost him his life. An invaluable man, Rube, but he overreached himself on this. He was too zealous. You see, I reasoned that, with Perlotti in the case and the snatch put on Mrs. Cartwright's corpse, there were professional criminals involved. That placed a different aspect on the whole matter. So, as you know, I put the Rube on the trail. This time he was too clever. Johnson's underworld pals got wind of what he was asking and tipped Johnson off that he'd better rub out the Rube. Johnson guessed that Rube was working for me, and you know all the rest of that episode."

"Yeah, yeah! Go on."

"Well, next there's the old lady's will. That was one of the really smart tricks Johnson pulled, only, of course, now it's been thrown out on the grounds of undue influence. The way I reconstruct it—and while Johnson's confession is somewhat vague on this point, I think a detailed study of its implications will bear me out—the old lady came to her trusted lawyer, to the man to whom she had given her power of attorney, to ask what to do about her blackmailing stepson. The lawyer says he can't act without knowing all the facts, so Mrs. Cartwright tells him. Now, what's a little matter of a breach of professional ethics to a man who is going to be disbarred anyway if his embezzlements are discovered, as they will be when the old lady dies and leaves the bulk of the estate to Gale, as it was under the old will? Adam Johnson knows the old lady's terror of publicity. He plays upon it, threatening her with exposure if she does not sign 'certain papers.' The poor soul is so frightened that she doesn't question—she signs! What she does is sign her life away, for those 'certain papers' are a new will. That in itself is a crude enough approach; the finesse lies in the terms of the will. Cy Handley, the old lady's only blood relative, is left a huge sum. The old will provided well enough for him, but by comparison it was a mere pittance. Johnson unquestionably figured he'd have Handley solidly on his side if the new will were ever contested. Gale, who loves her stepmother but is disdainful of money, is cut off with a neat hundred thousand dollars."

"You mean that that part in the will about Gale Cartwright being cut off for that 'all but one important instance' was pure invention on Johnson's part?"

"I do. But you must admit the cleverness of it."

"It's diabolical, knowing Gale as I do. I think she was hurt and bewildered more by what her stepmother had said than by what she had done."

"Well, that's all cleared up now. Then we turn to the largest bequest of all, the one to Jack Cartwright. The stepson must be dealt into the plot. As I've already told you, Johnson got Jack into his clutches by loaning him the money to pay Handley back."

"Money that came out of the Cartwright estate, I suppose?"

"Yep." The detective grinned at me maliciously. "And that's about the story of motives and opportunities. Want me to trace the methods of murder?"

"It might help!" I said, but the sarcasm was so heavy he dropped it without noticing. You have to hit Napoleon B. with a pile driver.

"Take the instance of old lady Cartwright. The method of murder was simplicity itself. The means of murder were far too involved, but you cannot have the former without the latter so I had better explain about the means of murder."

"Take your time, take your time," I groaned.

"All through the case I did not tumble to the means of murder beyond knowing that it was done by an air rifle. It was only Johnson's habit of 'saving' that tied the weapon to him at all. Many of us are like that, you know—savers who hate to part with any possession. In a way it was a death warrant for him if it were ever discovered, but then, *who* would ever find it or connect him with the murder of Mrs. Cartwright?

"He was right, too, up to a point. Of course I had one lead—the fact that an air rifle caused her death. Cy Handley manufactures such items. Undoubtedly, if there had been time I would have found out what we now know—that a workman at the Handley plant made weapons in his spare time and against company rules. One of the weapons he made in this way was an air rifle that looked like a golf club. He has identified Johnson as the purchaser. Brownlee found it in Johnson's bag at Briar Hill. It was such an ingenious weapon the old boy hated to part with it. Perhaps he thought he might have use for it again, maybe against Cy Handley who is an enthusiastic golfer. Johnson hasn't peeped on that subject. Possibly he'll set up a defense that the weapon was planted in his bag, but that won't hold water against the testimony of the workman."

"Sounds to me that you have that pretty neatly tied up," I said.

"I think so. Now, as for the method of murder, consider again the topography of this golf course. The sixth and seventh fairways are parallel along the first leg of the dog-leg seventh, with the rough of *Hell's Half-Acre* in between. Johnson has to take a chance, as most murderers do. He is reasonably bold. He tees up on the sixth and deliberately slices into the rough, *Hell's Half-Acre*. He says he'll play the ball, just as I did on the seventh. You thought me a damn fool, but you didn't think I was going down there to murder someone."

I admitted that I had thought of murdering him, but that was all. He let it pass.

"So his actions were perfectly normal to the foursome, as mine were to you." I refused to accept the challenge in his half-raised eyebrow. "The chance he took was that some other member of the foursome would slice into the rough with him and decide to play out also, but that didn't happen. Pearson, I discovered, offered to help look for Johnson's ball, but the lawyer said it was all right, he'd find it himself."

"Just like a thousand other golf games."

"Exactly. Nothing to stir the slightest suspicion. Adam Johnson did not even have a caddy; hardly ever used one, as a matter of fact, so that, too, was natural. Well, Johnson follows his ball into the rough of *Hell's Half-Acre* while the others start after their lies. Moving quickly, he takes out his golf club-air rifle, then stalks the old lady in her pitiful *Green Mansions* where he knows she will be taking her regular morning constitutional. His air rifle makes no noise as he shoots her, nor does she have time to make an outcry. He inspects the body to make sure she is dead and that the wound is so inconspicuous it is not likely to be identified as murder because of her known physical ailment. As a crowning stroke, he plays out his ball—a duplicate of the one he played into the rough. Tell me, would a man playing in and out of the rough like that excite your suspicion?"

"Not unless it was you counting your score," I cracked. "Maybe I might wonder at him finding his ball in such a spot."

"Okay, if you ask him that he simply tells you that he couldn't find it and played out another. What's your answer?"

Stymie!

The detective heaved a Napoleon B. sigh. "A clever, ruthless man." He shook his head in memory. "Almost a worthy opponent."

Oh, brotherrrr! Still, he *does* deliver the goods.

"Also, he had horseshoes all the way," Napoleon B. went on. "The means of murdering Jack Cartwright you already know. The method is obvious. Johnson went to remonstrate with Jack about drinking, to tell him he needed a clear head with me on the trail. But he could see that Jack was a very weak vessel, indeed. You can only condemn a man to one death, no matter how many murders he has committed. So—and I believe it was entirely on the spur of the moment—he shot his partner-in-crime."

"That doesn't gibe with what happened," I objected. "If it was on the spur of the moment, how come he planted Gale Cartwright's handkerchief in her brother's apartment?"

"It was actually one of those things that go to make a detective a hard and bitter old man at an early age. You will remember that Gale left Johnson's office with Handley. That handkerchief seemed an important bit of evidence. I felt that if Gale had lost it as she said, the logical man to have taken it was Cy Handley. The facts which I have now established are much simpler and more everyday.

"When Gale went out with Cy she dropped the handkerchief in the corridor. Johnson's male secretary found it and passed it on to the lawyer to return to his client. Now, killing Jack Cartwright in an unpremeditated manner and in a too great hurry, Johnson reached into his pocket for a handkerchief to wipe the fingerprints from Jack's gun. His fingers came out with Gale's handkerchief and, being a quick-witted man, he realized the possibilities, even while we were shooting the lock out of the door. He simply wiped the gun clean with Gale's handkerchief, dropped both to the floor, and fled. In the event that his fingerprints were found in Jack's apartment he could have covered that, too. He'd simply say he visited the apartment several times to discuss his client's business.

"As it happens, prints from Johnson were on file with the police as 'unidentified' in the Jack Cartwright murder, along with some others. But Cartwright's valet, a careful and conscientious servant, is willing to swear that he dusted the whole place thoroughly before he left that evening. So, there goes Johnson's alibi on that murder. The handkerchief he thought would help him will actually, through the testimony of his secretary, put him in the chair. The district attorney will probably charge him with the murder of Jack Cartwright, holding the charges of the murder of Mrs. Cartwright in abeyance in case a second trial is needed. He will realize that his strongest case, with the most corroborative evidence, is that involving the stepson."

"Trying to involve an innocent girl in fratricide was a pretty dirty trick," I said hotly.

The detective smiled at my innocence. "To love and war, Les, you can add murder as another thing all's fair in.

Besides, Johnson wanted to put Gale in a spot where she wouldn't ask awkward questions about the will. He couldn't count entirely on her distaste for money and the continuing shock of her stepmother's supposed duplicity as regards the will."

"The guy was turning into a one-man murder syndicate."

"Murder is a vicious treadmill, my friend. Once you're on it and have started the machine rolling, it's hard to get off. The smartest thing Adam Johnson did, apart from the will, was to finally hire professional killers as his accomplices. If he had to kill once, twice, there had to be other killings—mine, for instance. Yet, when you hire experts for murder you must expect to run up against experts who solve murders. That's axiomatic. Johnson knew it was only a question of time until I learned the entire truth. Hence the final attempt to rub us out. I'm still burned up about that."

"You're lucky it's figurative and not literal. It was the only logical move he would make with you closing in." I had been making notes on the little pad I always carry, lapsing into doodling when he spoke of things I already knew or had guessed. "He should have known you wouldn't walk into a trap like that without leaving someone to spring it once we were caught."

"By that time Johnson was close to insanity. He had come to believe himself omnipotent. I am convinced that Dr. Bryce would have turned up dead before long. That would have prevented awkward questions from Bryce, as an executor before and during probate of the will. As sole surviving executor, Adam Johnson could have juggled the accounts on such a large estate sufficiently to fool any auditors who were not looking for specific discrepancies. He could then have proceeded to milk the estate at his leisure."

"What about that business at the Cartwright mausoleum?" I asked, noticing he had said nothing about it.

There was a momentary lull. Then Napoleon B. Smith's face grew hard and taut. "Strictly underworld stuff," he said gruffly. "It almost paid off, too. Johnson was no better by then than a professional killer. It was kill, kill, kill, with him, to save his own lousy skin. Johnson knew, of course, that I was seeking an exhumation order. Knowing me, he realized I'd get it, too. There was only one thing to get the corpse out of the tomb. But that is not a one-man job. Johnson put his problem up to his gangster debtors. They suggested that there be a little grave robbery. Johnson admits he thought of the forged order from the coroner, and his allies considered it a wonderful scheme, one which would give them a loud, long laugh against their enemies, the police. To put the corpse the police were looking for into the morgue seemed a rare jest indeed! The order was forged by Harry the Pen, just as I had surmised."

"There seems to be no value in putting Mrs. Cartwright's body in the morgue, though."

"Sound, legitimate! Good business practice from the point of view of the criminal. Put the body in the morgue. A few days later, before somebody gets around to asking the coroner when he's going to hold an inquest on Margaret Jones, the 'mourning relatives' appear with another forged order, this time releasing the body into the custody of the bereaved ones for burial. Margaret Jones has a simple funeral—no fuss, no feathers, a plain wooden box, no headstone, the grass grows. What have you? It's damn good, when you think of it that way, Les; essentially simple, which is the beauty of every masterpiece, no matter whether it be a painting, a book, or a crime. But the simplicity did not enter until the professional hand was exposed. My one hope is that Adam Johnson will break down and implicate his gangster pals directly so that the ones who murdered the policeman with that booby-trapped coffin can get what's coming to them." Napoleon B. shook his head massively again.

"I would have handled the whole thing differently had I been Johnson, Les," the large man continued thoughtfully. "I would simply have hired Perlotti in the first place to do the job on the old lady. If Perlotti had been caught, he more than likely would have kept his mouth shut as to who had hired him. When you feel inclined to commit murder, Les, bear that in mind—employ a professional killer."

"I shall remember that," I told him sententiously, "the next time I feel an overwhelming urge to have you violently removed."

L'ENVOI

I closed my notebook with satisfaction.

"Wait a minute," Napoleon B. said to me. "I've told you all. How about a little true confession on your own? How's the state of your romance?"

"Wonderful!" I enthused. "Say, that girl is really something! Such a complexion! What eyes! What lovely hair!"

"Not to mention the shape she's in," he chimed in.

"That, too," I admitted.

"And the fact that she has several million dollars!"

"Huh? Who has?"

"Why, Gale Cartwright, of course."

I looked at him in amazement. "*That* creep!" I sneered. "Besides, she's marrying Cy Handley, although what she sees in that guy I don't know."

"Now, now, sour grapes," he admonished genially. "Who is the lucky lady, then? That gorgeous redhead from Dr. Bryce's office?"

Honest, sometimes Napoleon B. Smith gives me a pain.

"You sure are behind the times," I told him. "Right now, I'm preferring blondes. I'm talking about Sadie, the new manicurist at the Elite Barber Shoppe."

Oh, what the man said!

* * *

There we were at the seventh hole, the fateful dog-leg. Once again I was approaching par. All was right with the world. But I could not help feeling a tightening of the muscles as we walked to the tee.

I got off a nice drive, straight down the fairway about two hundred. The next shot would carry me around the dogleg neatly. I was satisfied.

The fat man stepped up to his ball.

"Better play it safe this time," I said maliciously.

Wham!

The ball sailed magnificently towards *Hell's Half-Acre*. For a moment it seemed it might clear the trees. Then it hit the top of a high pine and dived down amidst a small shower of needles into the *Green Mansions* of evil memory.

Napoleon B. looked after it. He addressed the ball . . . fervently. I said nothing, waiting. He took a half step towards the rough, hesitated. Then he turned to the caddy.

"Tee up another ball!" he growled, his tone daring me to say something.

"Playing three?" I inquired mildly.

He eyed me with an infinite, pitying scorn.

"You know very well," he said grandly, "that was nothing but a practice shot."

Then he topped one a wobbly but safe fifty yards down the fairway.

I hid a grin.

COACHWHIP PUBLICATIONS
COACHWHIPBOOKS.COM

THE GOLDFISH MURDERS

WILL MITCHELL

COACHWHIP PUBLICATIONS
CoachwhipBooks.com

**THE
SARA ELIZABETH
MASON
MYSTERIES**

MURDER RENTS A ROOM

THE CRIMSON FEATHER

COACHWHIP PUBLICATIONS
CoachwhipBooks.com

THE
SARA ELIZABETH
MASON
MYSTERIES

THE HOUSE THAT HATE BUILT

>>>> <<<<

THE WHIP

COACHWHIP PUBLICATIONS
CoachwhipBooks.com

THE
RUMBLE
MURDERS

Henry Ware Eliot, Jr.

KILL 'EM WITH KINDNESS

By
FRED DICKENSON

COACHWHIP PUBLICATIONS
CoachwhipBooks.com

A JUDGE MASSIE MYSTERY

THE CORPSE IS INDIGNANT

DOUGLAS STAPLETON
and **HELEN A. CAREY**

COACHWHIP PUBLICATIONS
CoachwhipBooks.com

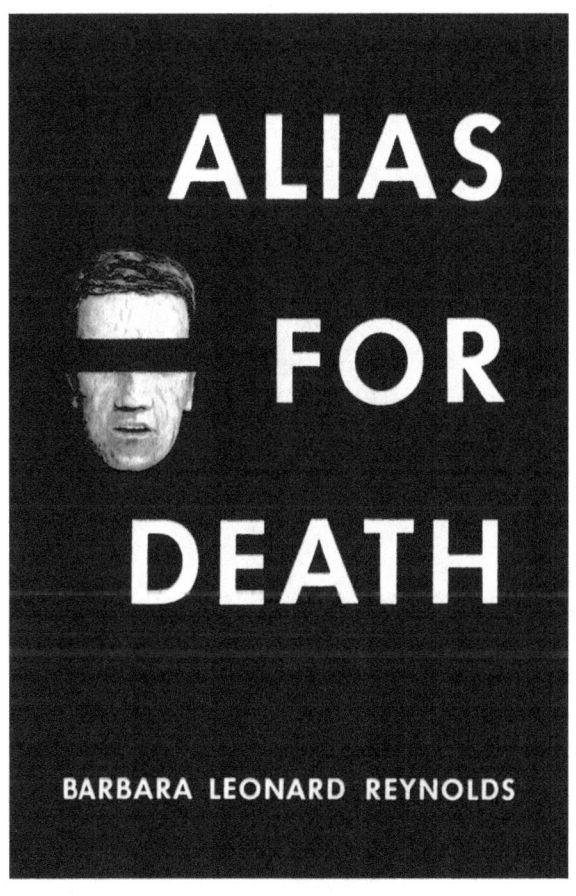

NARROW
GAUGE TO
MURDER

Carolyn Thomas

COACHWHIP PUBLICATIONS
CoachwhipBooks.com